# Far Beyond Fear

## "The Rise Of X"

Forest Eldine
Halvorsen IV

# DEDICATION

For all the wonderful people who have a fascination with the macabre.

# CONTENTS

*Fiction is a lure to the forbidden. It's an opportunity to experience a magical world with no limitations. It's like dreaming with your eyes wide open. Sometimes it's good....and sometimes it's terrible. To be able to really know the difference you must first be able to suffocate all of what you believe to be true ... you must exile your earthly understandings and limitations...put them to the side...we don't need them with where we are going......when we truly break that barrier we open our minds to a realm we never knew existed...we allow ourselves to travel and understand things brand new to us...like waking up on a new planet full of beautiful colors we have never experienced...sometimes when we break that barrier down we realize that what was once fiction to us is now a possibility...consider this if you choose to read any further....consider the world in which we live is a battlefield of good vs. evil things....a battlefield in which we have become completely desensitized to thus making some of us unaware of what team we are fighting for...we live in a world in which we demand immediate tangible proof or it doesn't exist... and when we are confronted with this idea....we consider it fictional...I ask YOU...yes...YOU reading this very page you silly willie, to throw out every earthly inherited product you consider to be fiction and fact ..throw it away and get on the spaceship....open your eyes to what is already in front of you and have a good laugh along the way...*

Thankful for the wonderful people in my life who have inspired me in some way or another to keep going. The ones who love me even though I am a head case. Taylor Halvorsen, Sophie, Khloe, My awesome sisters Tabi, and Lyndsey . Kristie, Adam, Kaylee, Maddie, Tyler,Nathan. My favorite music people Heartsick, Ghosts In Motion, Demonfband, Trivium, Creedence fu#$%^ Clearwater Revival…etc….

# WELCOME HOME

"Roll that damn window up, Victor. I am freezing my ass off over here," snarled Stanley with a keen sense of impatience in his freezing, hoarse voice. It had been a long cold car ride, and he could hardly bare the cold rushing into the car window anymore." Oh C'mon, man. Stop being such a weenie," Replied Victor. "We are there anyway.

Victor liked to mess with people and keeping them comfortable was not in his business. Stan and Vic had been friends as long as both could remember. All the way back to fifth grade when the boys would take turns pissin on the gym room doorknob hidden out of sight just before Mr. Quadner would unlock it to let the class out to third hour. The poor guy never noticed. One-time Quadner even popped a stick of gum in his mouth after touching the door knob to open the door. Stan had serious remorse for that, but Victor thought it was the funniest shit since Donny, the ADHD kid who's eyes were always bulged out got his teeth knocked out playing dodgeball.

Donny had tripped on his untied shoelace and nosedived into the hardwood gym floor. Donny hopped up and ran around in circles screaming manically holding his head and choking on his own blood. He looked like he had just swallowed a razor blade. The class formed a circle around the impact spot when they noticed one big, jagged tooth was sticking straight into the floor still, and the others laying scattered in a pool of DNA. The class was awe struck and had talked about that for years after the incident.

Victor was a little "rough around the edges" as one might say, the "alpha" of the two men barely into their twenties. Victor was like the alpha dog everyone in the pack followed, but also that one dog that would occasionally eat his own shit leaving the pack to question.

The boys were both twenty-one to be exact. Stan had a few months on Vic certainly, and it showed. But Victor would never admit that he was the younger of the two, overly confident and full of arrogance. Victor also had quite the potty mouth.

Both boys had completely distinct personalities, however they managed to cling to each other as best friends do. Suddenly both Vic, and Stan were caught off guard by the sudden smack of their own empty heads on the headliner of Victor's run-down Toyota. "Fuckin dirty old potholes" mumbled Vic.

That was typical of a central Michigan road in the middle of March. It didn't matter where you were in Michigan the roads were always full of behemoth potholes that would inevitably take its toll on even the newest of cars equipped with the best modern suspension manufacturing could provide. However, the moon surface of a road seemed excessively worse on Clark Street.

Clark street, would be the new road in which Vic, and Stan would travel daily to access their new rental house in the small town of Chesaning. Imagine driving in a M151A through an old mine field on the *Ho Chi Minh* trail back in Vietnam. That is what Clark Street was like.

"Fuckin A bud, here we are!" yelled Victor excitedly as he took a hard left into the gravel driveway causing both boys' shoulders to press into each other. Stan was still semi disoriented and chilled to the bone from Vic driving with his window down the entire 100 miles they just trekked from Muskegon to Chesaning. "Perfect timing! Look at that! the moving van is right in tow just as they promised," said Stan.

A large uhaul van huffed and puffed it's way to the entrance of the driveway coming from the opposite direction of Stan and Victor. Stan could see two men in the front seat who appeared to be of a different nationality. "Good thing they made it or I wouldn't fuckin pay em," said Vic. "Hell...I still might not anyways, more beer money baby". "First things first! I call dibs on the Jon! I have had to wizz like a cheetah this whole damn ride," said Stan.

"Somewhat of an excuse to escape Victors presence as fast as possible. Sometimes Stan had to take a series of small breaks from Victor to revive his ability to tolerate his presence. Stanley opened the car door hastily and considered kissing the ground, but didn't want to set off Vic. Victor wouldn't so much like the implication of being a bad driver. Stan already knew this from experience.

Vic shoved the old Toyota in park before coming to a complete stop. You could hear the parts clanking and grinding like a machine screaming for maintenance and repair, or an educated operator. This was standard of Victors daily driving. No regard to the vehicle whatsoever. Vic surprisingly appeared more excited than Stan had seen him in a long time. This new house was the change he had been longing for the past few years, and better yet he had his best childhood friend Stan as his roommate. Stan was the only other person on earth besides Victors parents who would tolerate his shit.

Deep down Stan just felt that Vic was excited to be in a town where nobody knew his bullshit. But he never would say that aloud, in fear Vic might pop him one right in the beak. Stan's door slammed with a jolting thud like thunder resounding in a valley, slightly pitching the car with Vic still inside. Before Vic could bitch him out about slamming his car door too hard, Stan had already been on his feet and halfway up the old driveway on to the old wooden porch. Stan in motion, noticed a pink flamingo statue with whitewashed eyes in the old overgrown flower bed just to the right of the deck. He thought it was God awful and could not wait to do some landscaping if the new landlord permitted. Vic watched Stan bust through the door as if he had lived there forever. Vic was slightly pissed off that the proprietor would leave the door unlocked. He shrugged it off. "Small town landlord for ya."

As Stan entered through the main door and into the living room, he immediately slowed himself down to look around and take it all in. Directly in front of him was the big living room, empty and baren. Behind the living room was the kitchen, on an open floor plan. He took a deep breath and embraced the smell of old hardwood floor as it rushed through his nostrils and into his empty head. (As Vic would say).

Stanley noticed the air was very thick, almost weighing him down. Stanley felt slightly odd about that but did not think much of it at that time. He was more enthusiastic for the new beginning. Stan had not actually seen the house in person before, only what Vic had showed him online. This was his first in person viewing. Victor had done all the negotiating with the proprietor over the phone. (Which wasn't much).

Stan guessed the bathroom entrance on his first try. It was the only door to the far left of the living room just passed the beautiful hardwood staircase. Stan skipped over and opened the heavy oak door to enter what appeared to be a normal everyday bathroom. A porcelain toilet on the left, a rust-stained sink on the right with trails of brown streaking the inside of the bowl, and a walk-in shower in the far back, all on top of a black and white checkered linoleum floor. "Simple," he thought. He closed the oak door behind him gently.

He now heard the rest of the guys now coming through the main door laughing and talking loud and obnoxious. The one grunt of the moving crew left behind to get the van doors open and start the crews heavy lifting. Stan unzipped his pants and began doing business as usual. "I can't believe this place is ours," he mumbled under his breath, watching as his stream of piss split in two and spattered droplets on the old flower wallpaper. Stan would come back later for sure he thought, and clean that up. Guys tend to do that. The arch enemy to woman.

Victor and the moving guys began what sounded like a small argument outside in the main living room. Stan could hear it faintly as he was finishing business in the little bathroom. He could tell it was the beginning of an intense argument just by the tone in Victor's voice, he knew it all too well.

"How do you not secure our property in the back of your moving van dip whad," yelled vic. Stan let out a sigh now piecing together more information as he eaves dropped. "For Christ's sake! You are a furniture moving businessperson! You should be good at this shit! Victor increasingly raising his voice as the reality set in.

 The moving company had apparently not secured anything in the back of their van before the trip stan presumed. The television, the glass coffee table, a bedroom set, and living room furniture all in a pile behind the moving van in the driveway.

As soon as their grunt had opened the back of the van door, a mountain of furniture and belongings had rushed out the back like an avalanche burying the grunt. That was a 100-mile trip with nothing secured. Their possessions must have bounced around like the shaking of a maraca.

Stan became pissed, or at least pretended to be, he was responsible for the hiring of this crew after all and knew that if he didn't tend to this situation that Vic would surely put all the blame on him. "How do you not hear that shit bouncing around," yelled Stan as he burst out of the bathroom buttoning up his trousers. "That must have sounded like Neil Pert ripping a drum solo." Stan peered past the moving crew (mostly foreigners) standing in the main doorway with pale white faces. He now could see the massive pile of belongings strewn about the driveway just as he imagined it seconds before.

He could see a set of work boots sticking out of the bottom of the pile kicking back and forth. Stan shook his head and wore the most pissed off face he could muster. Stanley had always felt it was hard to actually get angry, most of the time he would pretend to be mad just to appear normal. He felt it was an opportunity to attribute to his masculine image, or so he thought.

Victor lit up a Marlboro while shaking his head. "Better go dig your friend out," said Vic calmly as he slowly exhaled his first drag of the Marlboro. The boys were frozen in shock still. They did not budge.

"Well, get fucking moving boys!" victor yelled this time. The moving crew immediately sprang into action, and they headed out of the front door towards the mountain of furniture and possessions piled in the driveway ready to start assessing the damage and injury. Stan was sure their grunt would be okay. He could see his work boots wiggling up and down which told him he was at least still alive. Maybe suffocating, but at least alive.

"I'm embarrassed man!" what are the neighbors going to think if they see this shit!" said Stan as he looked Vic slightly above his eyes. Stan was afraid to make direct eye contact. Victor had quite the temper, and Stan was surprised Victor did not start swinging on the guys as soon as he discovered their fuck up. "Who gives a shit what they think, and it was you who hired them guys anyways," said Victor, throwing Stan a stern straight face. "Don't worry I fully intend to not pay them full price for this Vic. I WILL take care of it." Victor chuckled in disbelief.

Victor and Stan had signed a one-year lease on a house

that they had only seen mere pictures of online. The cheap price was a deal breaker for both. Six hundred a month for a two story, three bedroom, two and a half bath Victorian style house. The cherry on top was that it also sat on four acres of wooded forest. Stan had not believed the price at first after Vic showed him the photos of the place. It seemed too good to be true. But after a quick phone call to the landlord, they had legitimately come to believe that this was just that GOOD of a deal.

The landlord "Mike" had totally sold the deal to Vic, and Stan. Victor even managed to talk off one hundred dollars off the rent which was initially seven hundred. Mike had put much emphasis on the fact that the property was ready to be moved into anytime. Vic, and Stan were thrilled about that since they wanted out of the city immediately. Stan and Vic were far ready to get out of Muskegon Heights and away from the city life. Since they both worked for Stans dad's car business remotely, they decided it was time to get into a more rural, relaxed area where they seemed to think they would enjoy life better,

Victor slowly exhaled another drag of the Marlboro slightly smirking at Stan. Stan thought it made a unique smell mixed with the hardwood floors, he kind of liked it. "Well let's take a tour." "Shall we?" said victor. "Looks like we got a minute," said Stan.

They looked out the bay window and seen the crew had just dug their grunt out of the heap of mess and pulled him to his feet. He would live on to see another day. Victor chuckled and took in another drag of his half-smoked cigarette. Stan nodded his head to Victor and away they went.

They first decided to check out the second floor. Most of the downstairs was already visible being on the open floor plan. As they slowly walked up the solid oak staircase with a freshly polished floor, they were both awe-struck that this was actually their new place. A significant upgrade from the studio apartment they had both shared, that cost two hundred more a month in the city of Muskegon.

As they approached the top of the staircase, Stan looked back at Vic with an immense smile. "Can you believe this is ours Vic?!" the hallway ran straight from the top of the staircase to the far back end of the house. The first door on the left which was already open, opened to a big walk-in closet. Stan looked at Vic. "It's mine!" Victor didn't seem to mind at all and nodded in unusual agreement. Vic was sure he would also make out well and if not, he would certainly take whatever he wanted after the fact.

The next door about eight feet to the left from the first door opened into a beautiful large light blue bedroom that smelled of fresh paint. The sun cast beautiful rays through the crack between the curtain and windowsill. To stans surprise it already had a nice Bombay mahogany-stained dresser fully intact. Stan called dibs on this one immediately also. Especially being that he was suspicious his dresser had been damaged in transit as it was one of the last things the movers packed in the moving van. He was sure it had been on the bottom of the pile behind the van and had taken the full weight of the avalanche.

This particular bedroom also had a bathroom through another light brown hard oak door five feet to the right of the main door. Inside the bathroom was a rust lined sink, a sparkling white toilet, and a nice big shower with a blurry sliding glass door. Everything in this house was spotless and seemed to glee with sparkle. This room screamed Stanleys ownership.

Back to the hallway they both went. Stan 1, Vic 0. Vic stopped to admire the solid oak floor that ran through the entire upstairs hallway. The floor seemed to be freshly polished but had the smell of an old musty house still lingering. Vic did not mind the smell and was more thrilled at the appeal of this house.

The girls would definitely think he made more annually than he actually did, Vic thought to himself. Vic and Stan proceeded walking down to the last bedroom noting that it was oddly spaced out from the other rooms, roughly twenty feet from Stan's room and on the right side of the hallway. It seemed to be wasted space. The boys reached the third and final doorway. Vic smiled at Stan slowly turning his empty head to give him a grin. "You ready?" Victor turned the old crusty doorknob and pushed open the door. They were immediately slammed with what was an absurd rotten smell. The smell of sulfur, perhaps rotting eggs hidden under the floorboards.

"What the fuck is that!" said Vic sounding completely irritated again. "Of course, I get screwed and get the bedroom with the dead bodies hidden in the wall." Stan pulled his shirt over his snout trying with all his might not to laugh. "it's still a great room Vic! The room was painted a dark poop brown and had big black curtains smothering out all the possible daylight from outside. Stan really thought it looked like a turd with eyebrows on it. "Let's try to open a window and get a fresh breeze going in here Vic. I am sure the room just needs to air out." Stan let out a little cackle as he pulled the curtains open secretly pleased that Vic was paying his karmic debt to society. Thinking to himself that this was hilarious, and that Vic deserved the room that smelled like rotting eggs. After all he did drive 100 miles with his window down freezing Stan in the car. Stanley really didn't feel bad and was rather fulfilled when Vic gets the short end of the stick.

# SOMETHING STINKS

Vic and Stan, now back downstairs watched as the moving crew brought the last of their items in and stacked the last two boxes by the main door. The moving crew may not have been the best at securing their cargo, but they damn sure worked hard and fast. They must have been trying to make up for their little mishap, or they were scared as hell and wanted to get this job over with. Stan thought the latter. The cargo damage hadn't been as bad as they thought upon first glance. The TV miraculously hadn't been damaged in transit, and the extent of the damage appeared to be a few boxes that had the corners crushed in but the items in the box unscathed.

"Had that flat screen been damaged or my dresser, I wouldn't be paying you Jack!" said Stan. Victor sat with his eyebrows raised and his arms crossed dramatically rolling his eyes. He knew that Stan would go back on his word about not paying.

Stan had always been a nice guy and did not have it in his heart to shorthand the young moving crew. Stan reached his lengthy arm out and presented the movers a decent wad of cash. The movers were skeptical about the gesture. They remained still in silence; eyes wide. "Well come on and take it," said Stanley in a docile voice hoping to speed the process up. The oldest looking of the crew hesitantly inched forward as the room remained silent. The crew could feel Victors eyes tearing him limb from limb, they could sense his hatred and dismay for them all. Beads of sweat began dropping from his forehead as he slowly crept in to collect their pay. Stanley secretly admired his bravery.

Why couldn't I be more honorable like him Stan thought to himself. Finally after what seemed like a lifetime in silence the guy grabbed their cash and spun around. "Uh.. Thanks sir" he hesitantly mumbled under his foreign breath as they exited through the front door hastily.

"You pansy ass!" Vic said. "What man? they still did a good job, and nothing was actually damaged." "Mr. I'm not paying them blah blah blah.That was the perfect excuse to save some beer money for tonight you big hairy JACKASS, Said Vic in an indignant voice. "Whatever Vic! I'm over it.

"If you'll excuse me, I am goi.... BANG BANG BANG! Both Vic and Stan jumped out of their skin as three volatile thuds came from the upstairs in the room directly above them. Stanley thought he pissed himself and had to reach down and feel for a wet spot on his britches. Not this time, but he had actually tinkled himself a few times in the past when abruptly scared.

It sounded like it came from Victors new room. Three colossal thuds that felt as if it shook the entire earth. Very abrupt and disorienting like a mortar had just went through the window. Whatever it was did NOT sound happy. Dust slowly trickled down gracefully like a light snow settling on the shiny polished hardwood floor. Both roommates stared at each other with wide eyes. They just stared at each other as the last of the three thuds echoed away in the studs of the surrounding walls fainting away with a high-pitched ring. Stan thought for a second that it was possible a missile had just struck their upstairs ruining their fresh start. Maybe the moving crew shot a torpedo as they left stan thought to himself jokingly.

"Well, umm, that sounded like your room Vic, said Stan with a tone of apprehension but very matter of factly. "No shit, Einstein," said Vic. "Probably just that fucking window you opened idiot, probably blew some doors shut." Both Stan and Vic knew in the back of their minds that it was not the sound of a door shutting, not even the sound of a dresser falling over. That thudding was violent and in three concise bursts. It sounded like the noise of something intelligent.

Vic and Stan began creeping towards the stairwell both with clear apprehension on their faces. Stan could feel his heart pounding in his chest, like his heart was trying to break out of his rib cage and run away. Even being a daily jogger, Stan thought he would be able to sustain his heart rate better but that was never the case. His heart would beat hard and fast in any stressful situation.

Vic on the other hand seemed to maintain his composure but he still wore an unmistakable look of uncertainty, he could only fake it so much Stan thought. They both inched their way up the stairwell in silence as the last of the dust trickled down to the hardwood. Vic had whispered to Stan to stay put in case something, or someone was there. Vic quietly proceeded alone the last twenty feet to the last room on the right. Stan watched closely in fear.

Vic always played the tough guy roll and it drove Stanley nuts. Stan watched as Victor stopped the last foot from the open door just before he would be visible to anyone, or anything that may be in the room. Victor took a quiet deep breath which almost made him blow chunks immediately. There was that fucking rotten smell again, Vic thought. Like a giant rotten egg stretched over his nose. At this point he was terrified inside of what the hell was going on but he played the role well. Something just simply did not feel right. The air seemed to have a weight to it, a sudden thickness. Vic began to curl his fists into a ball, he was ready to take the last step and see what or who could possibly make them explosive thuds on the floor. Just as Vic began to take his last step, he was stopped immediately in his tracks by the sound of the doorbell ringing and a young kid saying something neither Stan, nor Vic could make out.

Vic viewed this as an opportunity to be the element of surprise and he charged into the bedroom fists balled and raised. "You want some o this mother fucker" he said as he did a quick 360-degree sweep. The room was completely barren. "Not a fucking thing" he mumbled. He looked around a second time as the flow of relief took over his heart rate again. He brought his fists down and cleared his face of his best tough guy look.

He felt like he looked like a golden glove boxer when he pretended to be tough. Stan thought he looked more like a jailbird who had done a few too many stints in the drunk tank down to the county jail. A total sleaze ball. The closet was wide open, and he could see that nothing was there. Completely empty and barren just as he had left it. All that remained was just that awful rotten smell, and poop-colored walls.

Vic let out a stress laugh, being scared was not something he usually became a part of. Releasing his clenched fists Vic spun around and started walking fast to the hallway where he could now hear Stan taking up a conversation with what sounded like a young teenager. "What the hell does he want"? Yelled Vic in a hoarse voice interrupting purposefully. Stan already began closing the door and now had a pale white face. More pale than usual Victor thought. "Some random kid….he told me to stay out of the coal room," said Stanley looking completely bamboozled.

# PETES PLACE

 Stan, and Vic entered the pubs main door ready as ever
now to get their drinks on. If they get lucky, maybe they
will get a temporary "roommate" Stan thought in the back
of his head. The six block walk to the bar would be worth
it either way he thought, just as long as they both could get
a little stress relief. "My bed isn't even set up...what the hell
is she going to sleep on if I get lucky." He rapidly and
mentally equated that the throw down sleeping bag would
suffice. After all, any lover who goes home with him for a
one-night stand, probably isn't worried about my actual
bed. And he probably shouldn't be worried about her too
much either.
Stan took a quick view of the bar from the main doorway
realizing that it was in fact a dive bar as he suspected.
A large barren room with a typical looking bar, two pool
tables, and a nice-looking juke box directly across from the
billiards tables. The suspended ceiling was full of bends
and dips along with brownish black water stains. Some
portions of the suspended ceiling had duct tape holding it
at the seams. It was your everyday dive bar.
Vic led the way across the empty dance floor to the bar. It
appeared to be completely open. Not a single person sat

on the black and white checkered bar stools. Who Stan assumed to be the bar tender had his back turned to them and was leisurely washing dishes. The dishes clanked gently as the man gracefully moved his sponge back and forth. The neon lights flickered in the entrance window. Stanley liked the green one. "Pete's Place" it said. "What a fucking bust man" Vic thought. He and Stan had two different views on this place. But it still was not going to steer him away from getting a nice buzz and cranking some good music on that old jukebox he had seen across from the pool table.

 Stan and Vic both grabbed a seat, leaving enough space between them for if they get "lucky." That was like guy code. Don't sit directly next to each other on the bar stools to leave space for a female. "Double shot of Vodka," Stan said to the old man who he assumed was the bartender.

The old man who had his back turned washing dishes spun around and immediately Vic and Stan froze in their seats. The old man appeared to be blind in his left eye, that particular eye a complete shade of white. Absolutely terrifying facial features. Leathery skin and sink holes for eye sockets his attire representing that of a butler.

Both Stan and Vic hesitated in what to say. The old man didn't even say a word, he slowly grabbed the house bottle of Vodka with his shaky hands staring them down and poured up a double shot, his hands shaking as if he was ready to burst out of his skin.

Stan hesitantly slid two, one-dollar bills across the bar with his left hand, on the slide back he brought forth the freshly poured double shot of vodka noticing it felt slightly chilled to the touch. Most likely from sitting in this dark dungeon all day.

The bartender produced a mischievous smile and began to laugh in his old man voice uncontrollably. "Got you fellas good!" "Not every day I get to prank a newcomer, lots of usuals in this place." "All the same faces, same day, and same time." "Except when Ms. Caldwell didn't show up on

Tuesday last week." "Turns out she had a mean stroke and didn't make it. "What a shame." Vic laughed a little in disbelief that this old man had a sense of humor. "Double shot for me too bud" said Vic in a chipper voice. Now feeling relieved that this old man wasn't some sort of secret monster waiting to pounce them and tear their flesh apart after they get loose with a few drinks.

Stan took a look around the bar taking it all in. So far it seemed to be a normal looking dive bar. Brown wooden walls, neon signs, and the smell of aluminum cans and puked up cigs. He decided next he would try make some conversation and learn a little of the town.

"Nice to meet you sir, I'm Stanley, and this is my childhood friend/roommate, Victor." "You can call me Stan for short, and Victor, Vic."

"What shall we call you good sir?" The old man hesitated for a quick second and then replied "Peter, but Pete for short."

The old man slid a double shot over to Vic. Both Stan and Vic raised their shot glasses. "Cheers to Peter" They clicked their glasses together making a glasslike ringing sound and both swallowed their doubles in one quick opening of the throat. They both busted out in laughter barely managing to finish swallowing their alcohol. They were like high school kids anytime someone used the word "Peter".

"Whoop" yelled Vic with a bright smile on his flushed face. "Feel the burn" Stan tucked his chin into his throat as he sucked down the last bit of Vodka from his mouth. He thought after years of drinking with Victor it would eventually get easier. But this was not the case. It still tasted like jet fuel every time.

"Better get the tunes going" Vic mumbled under his breath as he hopped from his stool to go over to the jukebox with an arrogant sway of his body. As Vic dug into his pocket to pull out some change, the bars main door flew open.

Three gorgeous women walked in as if they owned the place, laughing out loud and swinging their hair around to make a big scene. All Victor could hear in the back of his head was the tune "cherry pie" and the motions of the woman all seemed to play in slow motion in perfect harmony to the song. Vic put his change back into his pocket, with an immediate game plan he proceeded back to his bar stool. He didn't want to blare music too loud and ruin the chance of him conversing with one of these women. Or take the risk of playing the wrong music. This would take some work. Vic arrived back at the bar. "Look at that" Vic whispered to Stan with a huge smirk on his face. "Looks like this is going to be a good night after all little buddy.

The three girls had journeyed to the far end of the bar where they began undressing their coats, scarfs, and hats. The boys watched in total amazement in what seemed to be slow motion show as they undressed. Stan and Vic both imagining them taking it all off. Stan preferred the blonde on the far left, and Vic was a fan of the red head. To Vic the brunette would be a backup in case he didn't have such luck with the red headed girl.

The bartender floated over to serve the woman up as they all became entertained in conversation never seeming to notice Stan, or Vic eye-fucking them from across the table. Stan and Vic both hurrying to get their bearings, they were to waste NO time in this campaign. Like two animals in heat. Stan heard the main door swing open again and looked behind him noticing two large built men in biker apparel enter the bar with brute arrogance. One of them had a black leather vest on with white print reading "Hells Wheels", which Stan would later find out was a self-proclaimed biker gang from Chesaning.

The men went directly to the pool table as they probably did every night Stan assumed. He didn't think much of it other than noticing their dramatic tough guy entrance. Victor had not taken his eyes off the girls since they settled into their seats. It appeared to Stanley he may have been even drewling. But Stan wasn't really surprised.

"Okay little buddy, I'll go first, keep an eye on the situation." "If I look like I'm struggling, then come bail me out" said Vic with total confidence that plan would work. Victors' demeanor reminded Stan of when they were young boys creating battle plans in the sandbox with their toy soldiers, excited and full of energy. Vic slammed his second double shot and put his game face on.

Stan tried not to laugh as he watched Vic strut his ass across the bar to talk with the woman. Vic appeared to have his right shoulder slightly leaning down and tipped back. He had one eyebrow raised and a little pep in his step. Stan thought he looked like a total goon. If anything, they will admire him for his courage since he clearly looks like a fucking nerd.

Stan watched out of the corner of his eye as Vic made contact. The girls all stopped talking and had little smiles with slightly blushed faces. Stans face was just as red, he was cringing like watching an episode of Jerry Springer, it's unbearable to watch but you just can't help it. Vic threw his chin up and placed his hand on his right hip perhaps showing his "confidence".

As soon as Vic opened his mouth to speak, the butt of a pool stick came ramming right into his left cheek making a fleshy sound that Stan could hear even across from the entire bar. The guys playing pool had not been aware of Vic. As far as they were convinced, they owned the entire bar and typical situational awareness did not apply to them. You watch out for them, not the other way around.

Stan suddenly busted out in laughter; he could not contain himself. Vic rolled his head side to side grabbing his cheek in disbelief. Slightly dazed and in embarrassment. His face burning bright red. Stan immediately got up and sprung across the bar to bail him out. After all, that was the initial plan Victor created.

"Vic, man are you alright?! Stan yelped before he completely made it over to Vic. The pool guy who hit Vic seemed to not think it was a big deal at all. "Hey bud, you gotta watch where yer walking," said the biker guy in a slight accent Stan couldn't quite put his finger on. Must be Chesaning talk Stan thought, a little hillbilly and a little normal mixed into one. Stan did agree that Vic had walked into that one willingly, but still not an apology for Vic. Stan grabbed Vic by the arm "Lets get moving man." Vic with nothing to say followed in tow. Holding his cheeks in disbelief still. "How could this happen to me" he thought to himself. "I am the lady master!" (Or so he thought.)

"That was a fucking tragedy Vic," said Stan. Vic took his seat at the bar like a defeated little chap. Vic looked over at the pool guys. Maybe had that guy not been 6'3" and solid built, Vic might have had something more to say to him. He let it go. Vic looked at Stan. As soon as they both made eye contact, they both busted out laughing. "That was pathetic man" said Stan amongst his laughing. "That should have been you said Vic.

# LUCKY RUBBER

The guy's laughter was suddenly interrupted by what sounded to them like a porn stars soft angelic voice. "Excuse me sir." (Little giggle) "I think you dropped this sir" (her voice was really in a diplomatic clear manner nothing of sexual gesture). Vic turned around to see the beautiful red headed girl shyly batting her eyes at him and holding her hand out. As Vic looked down, he was immediately red in the face all over again and embarrassed as ever when he recognized what she was holding out for him to repossess. It was his fuckin lucky condom he had kept in his pants pocket for the last three years.

It even went through the washer a few times, but Trojans seem to hold up apparently, especially the little size. "Oh yeah...Uh thanks miss" said Vic as he haphazardly took the condom back quickly trying to figure out how the hell this thing fell out of his pocket. He wasn't as surprised considering this seemed to be his usual luck in life. Always getting embarrassed. But still in his heart of hearts. He was "a ladies' man."

Vic returned the condom to his other pocket assuming the other one must have had a hole in it. "I'm Vic." he said sticking his right hand out for a shake. "Sarah" she replied.

She didn't seem to be interested in the handshake for some reason, but this didn't offend Vic surprisingly. She waived her other two friends to come over. They had been sitting across the bar observing the altercation with little smirks on their faces talking back and forth under their breath. The other girls quickly hopped off their bar stools and strutted their way. Stan awkwardly interrupted in an obnoxious voice he didn't intend to muster. "I'm Stan, nice to meet you." He awkwardly stuck his hand out again only to also be rejected by Sarah.

"These are my best friends," said Sarah pointing to the brown-haired girl, and the other blonde. "I'm Jessica, but you can call me Jess," said the brown-haired girl. "And this is Maggie," she said introducing Maggie for Maggie. Maggie gave a bashful little smile and waived. Both Vic, and Stan were ecstatic inside but trying to play it cool and act calm. Both guys were certain they were in for a good night and now that everyone is on a first name basis Vic decided to start the party.

"Double shot of Vodka for everyone in the group" said Vic boldly leaning over the bar looking at the bar tender who returned a slight comical smile. Peter the bartender knew these girls very well, they were regulars at the bar HOWEVER they were NOT drinkers. They usually traveled to the bar in a group and ate lunch together. Never had Pete ever seen them party. Not even once. "Oh, we don't drink," said Sarah cutting Victor off in a sense. "We are just here for Pete's delicious cooking, and we like to meet newcomers of the town, and this is a good place to do just that.

Vics heart sank as he realized his chances of getting laid probably went from slim, to impossible. Stan didn't seem to care; he was getting rather quiet and looking a little tired from the move. Stan had already given up before even trying. "We would love to talk and get to know you guys though; we are ambitious to meet the newcomers of Chesaning."

Vic, still holding on to a splinter of hope, and slightly in denial that his chances of getting laid were reduced to dust in the wind, replied with a choked voice, "Sure, that sounds good." "Still a double shot for Stan and me, Pete. Pete nodded his head and started pouring up the shots right away. Pete was definitely enjoying the show. Vic looked at Sarah and started in conversation, "we are new here, we just moved here from Muskegon Heights." "The heights they call it." "Just arrived today."

"Stan and I don't know much of anyone, we got thirsty and decided we would check out the town tonight." "That's great," said Sarah. "Do you usually drink vodka when you're thirsty?" The girls giggled in the back.

"We don't get a lot of newcomers, and when we do, they don't stay very long." "What side of town are you guys staying on?" chimed Jessica joining the conversation for the first time. "Over on Clark Street," replied Stan hoping to get more involved in the conversation.

Pete served up the boys their third round of double shots. "Vic, and Stan both could feel the buzz starting to kick in. Vic feeling a little more comfortable in his own skin now was still going to try and put the moves on Sarah. "What house on Clark Street, said Jessica very interested now with a serious look on her face. "The only red brick house on the street, "replied Stan. All the girls gave each other a serious look. "That's an old house, lots of history," said Sarah. "Lots of people come and go in that one." "Rumor is that it's inhabited with evil spirits." "Local pastor wouldn't even go to do a cleansing on the house for the last tenant, said it was too powerful for him to deal with again."

Vic, and Stan both felt their heart sink, immediately thinking of the things that have already happened the first few minutes of arriving. "Last time I'll sign a fuckin lease without seeing the house in person first," thought Vic. "I don't believe our land-lord mentioned any of that to us," said Stan in a strange professional sounding voice. Vic knew that Stan talked like that only when he was nervous. "Lots of people have died in that place, and back in the 30's it was a funeral parlor." Sarah informed.

"The Parker family was murdered in that house by "The nun," said Jessica. "Don't think they ever caught her either. Little Timmy Parker had written down in his dying moments "Lady in the hood, nun, killed us".. they found him slumped over the table in a pool of blood." "They could barely make out the writing there was so much blood" Jessica could see the sheer terror in the boys' eyes. And to Vic he thought she was oddly enjoying it.

"Well, that's enough fucking ghost stories for me!" Vic snapped his finger at Peet. "One more double for the road old timer, we got some unpacking to do." Vic abruptly stood up and started putting on his jacket signaling Stan with a quick finger snap to do the same. Pete slid down a double and Vic drank it just as fast as it came. "Nice meeting you wonderful ladies" said Stan trying to play it cool. The situation had become completely awkward for everyone. Vic remained silent as he raised his eyebrows in frustration. Apprehensive that he now lives in a fucking haunted house. A haunted house that had already started giving him problems.

"Aww, not goanna stay for dinner?" said Sarah with a slight hint of laughter in her voice" Vic thought she seemed rather satisfied with this whole conversation and he found it pretty strange. "Not a fucking chance man!" Vic grabbed Stans shoulder and looked at the ladies. "Could've had a good time…but instead you ladies want to tell ghost stories…hmmm…what a strange town this is indeed." Vic threw cash down on the bar for Pete, a crisp twenty-dollar bill. "Keep the change, Pete." Pete nodded his head and scooped up the twenty-dollar bill silently. Vic and    Stan    both    headed    for    the    door.

# GHOST STORIES

"What the fuck man" said stan as soon as they exited the bar door refreshed by the cold crisp winter air. "This place gives me the fucking creeps," said Vic. "Let's just walk home and forget this even happened." "So much for getting some action." Stan and Vic walked home in silence down the dark sidewalk. Both knowing all too well that this house is more than likely haunted considering all the things that had happened the first few minutes of moving in. Vic didn't want to accept it. He always thought that people who tell ghost stories are fucking looney. Now he was second guessing inside and wondering if he himself was letting his imagination get carried away.

"Let's keep to the plan," said Stan. "We are going to be just fine." "No ghosts are going to hurt us, and as for the murders…well that's just something that happens unfortunately." "We don't even know if that's true yet." Vic nodded his head in agreement thinking that he was certainly going to check records at the public library about this. But the pit of his stomach turned, and he had a deep gut feeling that they had big problems ahead of them. The boys walked in silence. The only sound was the muffled thudding of their sneakers as they proceeded forward.

After a cold and quick six blocks Vic and Stan reached the property line of their new house. Vic immediately feeling that same thick, heavy feeling he felt when they first entered the house earlier. Quickly he tried to shrug it off as they were heading up the driveway. "Fuck this ghost shit man, this is our house, and we are the ones living in it." Vic said this with the arrogance he got from drinking Vodka. Liquid courage. But deep inside he felt the doom surrounding them. They both could.

Both boys knew this wasn't turning out as they had planned it. As they approached the front door both boys simultaneously stopped. Dead silence. Not a peep of light shimmered in the house whatsoever and not the faintest sound of traffic in the distance. Sheer darkness swallowed them up like a black hole. Both Stan and Vic could feel that immense feeling you just can't explain. That feeling when sheer terror and doom over run your soul, and the chills run up and down your spine. The kind of feeling that steals all your comfort.

Vic and Stan gave each other a grim look when they reached the end of the driveway, making eye contact for once. Something Stan didn't usually do as he felt inferior to Vic. Vic reached in his right pocket and jingled for their new keys. Stan waited as Vic ran sacked all his pockets, noticing that his right front pocket had a big hole in it as he suspected. Pocket change in his left pocket jingling like Santa's sleigh. Vic became enraged, "You are fucking kidding me!" At this point Vic was throwing all his stuff that remained in his pockets onto the small deck.

Lucky Trojan condom, and a half-smoked pack of Marlboros, also lots of loose change. Cursing and tired he discovered that he did not have the keys one hundred percent, matter of fact. He remembered that he had dropped his stupid condom earlier and had a sense that the keys may be lying on Peters bar floor. "The keys have to be back at the bar," said Vic in a panicked voice. "It's alright man, let's just find another way inside tonight, and we can go see Pete tomorrow." "We can check the sidewalks in the morning too when the sun comes up." "Hopefully nobody would take them."

Stan slightly taking over the situation, urged them both to walk around the house and try for an unlocked window, who knows, perhaps the back door would be open, especially since the landlord left the front open. Stan and Vic stepped off the front deck into the tall uncut grass. "Fuck man, it is really dark out here," said Vic in a nervous voice. "Hopefully I don't get no fuckin tics," said Victor. "It's fucking March you city slicker." "You're not going to get tics this time of year," said Stanley.

"What is that ?!" Stan abruptly redirected Vics attention to what appeared to be a cellar door in sight as they rounded the east corner of the house. Vic and Stan both surprised to see this access door to a cellar. The Landlord had never mentioned a cellar entrance. Stan and Vic standing outside the newly discovered cellar door noted that the same rotting smell was seeping out from this door that had been emanating in Victors new room.

Vic feeling tired and ready to just get into the house and get set up for bed reached down for the Cellar door and grabbed the right-side handle. With a first try tug at the door it didn't budge. "Fuck!" Vic explosively began curb stomping the cellar door as it made a horrendous loud booming noise that seemed to echo into oblivion in the cellar. He had no such luck opening it this way. Vic reached down a second time in blind rage and grabbed both doors this time.

He tugged violently with all his might. The rage of bi-polar personality kicking in. Still nothing budged. Stan feeling uncomfortable when Vic gets this angry decided to give it a try himself. Stan reached down to the right-side door and grabbed the handle. Vic in the background cursing up a storm losing his temper. Stan turned the handle and Vics cursing was halted by a loud metal grinding, sliding noise. Vic immediately realizing all he had to do was turn the damn handle before yanking on the damn thing.

Stan pulled up as the door released. A cold rush of air that smelled of rotting eggs rushed into their nostrils. Both boys immediately began scrunching their faces and trying hard not to gag. "Man, something is dead inside this house…maybe they didn't bury all of the Parkers old crusty bodies," said Vic as he now had his shirt pulled up over his nostrils.

Stan remained silent realizing that they now had to hike their way through a dark stairwell that was completely full of thick cobwebs, and absolute blackness. Stan couldn't see a damn thing they were waking into, but they knew that they had to try their way into the house through this God forsaken hell hole. "I'll go," said Stan knowing all too well that Victor was already on his last thread. Stan didn't want to burden him anymore with frustration. Typical behavior of a submissive in an egotistical friendship.

"Be my damn guest…" replied Vic as he inched backwards a little bit trying to avoid the gnarly breeze of rotting carcass that was escaping out of the old cellar. Stan grabbed for a medium sized stick off the ground. He decided that stick would be best for removing the thick cobwebs in front of him. He stuck the stick in and gave it a twirl, just like a cotton candy wand wrapping hundreds of cobwebs onto the stick. It wouldn't get all of them. But he would at least be able to head into the cellar without a mouthful of cobwebs.

Stan took his first step into the cellar; he could feel his heart racing out of his chest. He hated when he volunteered to do tough guy shit. He always regretted it soon after he embarked. Only two steps in, Stan had accumulated enough cobwebs around the stick to make it look like an oversized cotton candy wand. A disgusting brown one. The kind you wouldn't ever dream of eating. Spinning it straight in front of his face, clockwise, and counterclockwise. Vic started to chuckle. "You look like a fucking Harry Potter," Ha-ha. Why don't you say a cute little spell and light this place up Stanley boy? Stan chuckled pretty hard at that one. "Abra ...fucking cadabra. "Said Stan playing the role laughing. As soon as he took another step,

both boys heard a massive thud from a spot of the house they could not determine. Stan turning around to look at Victor, hoping he was just playing a joke. But he knew the look on Vic face was a serious one. After all these years of knowing Vic and being friends, he could tell just what he was feeling by facial expression and demeanor. Stan and Vic were certainly scared shitless. "Hello!" Vic and Stan heard a woman's voice say. Bang, Bang, bang! Vic realized that someone was knocking around the corner of the house at the front door.

"FRONT DOOR!" Said Vic. Both boys took off around the corner, Stan's hair full of cobwebs. Vic came around the corner first. Victor was the fastest of the two and aways had been. Stanley still clinging to the cotton candy wand. It somewhat reminded him also of the giant meaty drumsticks depicted on the flintstones program. Stanley threw the drumstick off into the tall grass watching as the cobwebs stuck it to the top of the grass slightly drooping the grass towards the ground.

At the door was Sarah from the bar, holding up his set of keys smirking as she jingled the side to side. She appeared to be thrilled stan thought. It was very odd.

"Forgot something did ya?" Pete was just about to close the bar when he found them. "Figured they was yours since the other thing had fallen out ya know." Vic snatched the keys from Sarah. "Thank you!" Said Stan before Vic could open his mouth and say something rude. We were just about to find a way in through the cellar. "Through the cellar.?"

Sarah looked down with a serious look on her face. "That's not a good place to be, I wouldn't be down there if

I were you...." "And just why the hell would that be!?" Vic busted with an intense look on his face. "That's where he remains..." Oh Stop it with your fucking ghost stories Sarah! Yelped Victor. "You're just trying to scare us out of here". Sarah didn't respond with anything audible, instead she shrugged her shoulders, and tilted her head to the side giving both boys the impression that she really didn't care if they believed her or not.

# I DON'T EAT MEAT

"I think you better go," said Stan in a disappointed sounding tone. "We've had a long day and we still haven't settled in." "Thanks for bringing our keys back though, we owe you a burger." "Yuck, no thanks, said Sarah." I don't eat meat..."

She gave Stan a repulsed look with her eyebrows raised, she then spun around and headed off the deck to walk home. Stan watched Vic as he stared at her rump bouncing up and down as she walked away. Her thick thighs rubbing together with each step made the fabric of her blue jeans swipe together creating a gentle whooshing sound. Vic was a dirty dog, no doubt about it.

What a bizarre encounter Stan had thought to himself. Awkward, and short lived. This whole situation is ridiculous. Stan had no idea how far Sarah could've gone out of her way to bring them keys, but either way the girl had to be trying to help, right? But why would she keep telling crazy stories about this house.

Stan was in a tired state of confusion and decided it was best to give this thought up for the night. Vic produced the skeleton key and shoved it into the dead bolt lock. Tt turned with a slow eerie metal on metal scraping noise, followed by a sudden click. "Ahh, finally," Victor mumbled with the slight sound of relief in his voice. Both boys proceeded into the dark doorway from outside. Stan noted the smell of polished hardwood floor mixed with an old musty smell again. It sort of reminded him of an old moist library book that sits on the shelf for twenty years without being touched. Probably just as this book will be in time. Oddly enough Stan kind of liked that smell.

"I'm going straight to bed, just going to crash out on the floor man, I am exhausted, Said Victor. Stan closed the front door and locked back up the deadbolt following Vic up the stairs to the hallway. The moonlight beamed through the window at the far top end of the stairs providing enough light to navigate in the dark. Just enough to make out the outline of things. A houseplant sitting directly in front of the window in the sill, cast small broken shadows amongst the hallway floor, like black intricate veins running through the floorboards. The plant looked to be a Tineke rubber tree thought Stan, but he couldn't tell for sure. He couldn't recall noticing the plant in the daylight on their first trip through the house earlier.

"Well, I will see you in the morning," said Stan as he stopped next to his doorway right at the top of the steps. Victor continued and mumbled something under his breath that Stan couldn't understand. Stan didn't care. He just assumed that Victor had too many double shots of Vodka. "Nothing new" Stan thought to himself grabbing hold of his doorknob. He noticed immediately how cool the doorknob was to the touch. Seemed much colder than a usual doorknob. He slowly turned the knob popping the door open. Stan could hear Victor open his door and shut it right after. It dawned on Stan that neither Vic nor himself had even stopped to grab the sleeping bags out of the massive pile of belongings shoved in the living room area.

Stan began immediately regretting being lazy and not taking care of a few things before getting drinks. He had always been a procrastinator. The brick house was never built with actual light fixtures in the ceiling. Only a floor lamp, or table side lamp could be plugged in, and you were lucky to have an outlet in the room you were in. Stan would have to go back downstairs if he wanted a sleeping bag, and he was sure that it would take some searching in the dark new house. Something that did not directly appeal to him.

He would have to feel around the walls while on his hands and knees for an outlet. Even with the bedroom door open and moonlight peering in through the double pan window he couldn't get enough light from the hallway to see it at first glance from the top of the stairwell. Stan let out a sigh. "Fuck me sideways," he mumbled under his breath and shrugged his shoulders…He wasn't too thrilled to have to navigate back down the stairs all alone this time. Stan suddenly froze and remembered a time when he was in a similar situation. Total flashback of trauma.

With a quick burst of heat and flushed cheeks he immediately reminisced about the time when he was twelve years old with his friend's family at their cottage for the weekend. He had been very apprehensive about this trip and had a raw gut feeling that something would absolutely go wrong. Stan typically didn't do well staying overnight at other friends' houses. Many times he had to call for his parents in the middle of the night to come rescue him. But for whatever reason he had agreed to go with his friend Chris to their cottage for an entire weekend.

He had hoped after agreeing to the trip that his parents would then dispute his eagerness to travel, but they thought it was a wonderful idea. Stan let out a deep breath and closed his eyes standing in the dark hallway, he could remember it all.

On the first night of the trip Stan had magically managed to fall asleep, which falling asleep was the hardest part. If you could manage that, you were basically in the clear. After a few short hours of light sleeping Stan suddenly woke up in his sleeping bag in total distress. While lying on his friend's bedroom floor in a state of desperate confusion, he was immediately overcome with the sensation of having to take a number two. The worst sense of urgency he had ever experienced, it was painful, like a bowling ball had been dropped on his abdomen.

He flew up, surprised that he hadn't shit himself moving from the horizontal position to upright. "This is bad," thought Stan. This was the most horrendous feeling of urgency he had ever experienced in his twelve years. Of course, this would happen to him in the middle of the night while he just so happened to be at a friend's house. He had no time to think about anything other than locating the toilet in the dark and not waking anyone up.

How embarrassing would that be, he thought. Embarrassment is the arch enemy to a young boy's ego, he couldn't take another blow, he had to resolve this unfortunate situation. Clenching his butt cheeks as tight as he could and looking around the dark room, Stan picked a direction, and away he went. It was complete darkness and silence, this would be a guessing game in which he could not afford to fuck up. Finding in front of him after traveling just five feet, what appeared to be a doorway to what Stan hoped and prayed was the hallway.

He proceeded waddling through whatever opening he had just found with both hands behind him helping clasp his cheeks together. His stomach now began growling harder than ever. Beads of sweat started to drip from the pores of his forehead. "NO TOILET", he said aloud as the panic set in even worse than before. He urgently began looking around side to side only to see nothing in the darkness. Stan became incredibly nauseous, and felt as if he was going to explode.

Stan was running out of time; he picked another direction and just went for it. C'MON...C'MON!! thought Stan. Panic made his heart race and now he was starting to feel defeated. He thought he might actually shit himself and have to wake someone up to assist him with his mess. Stan stopped suddenly to pinch with all the might he could muster. He just couldn't carry on. His calve muscles throbbed and Charlie horsed, and he stood on the very tip of his toes squinting and holding his breath. SPLAT!! His worst nightmare came rocketing out his gym trouser with a deep thudding noise. Kind of like if you dropped a russet potato on a gym floor, followed by liquid popping and bubbling noises. Eyes wide in shock, Stan slowly looked down only to find the outline of the worst site he had ever seen before.

"The smell!," he thought. It was unlike anything he had ever smelled before. Like something rotting in the stagnant waters of the everglades. He was in total shock. How could this happen? Stan looked forward only to notice something moving across the room in the shadows. "Stan is that you?" he immediately recognized the soft voice of his friend's mother.

Stans heart dropped. Not only did he manage to crap himself. He crapped himself right by his friend's mother's bedside. He wasn't even close to a bathroom. The mess was everywhere, like an all-brown Picasso painting. Stan felt like a criminal who just got caught robbing a bank.

They later found out his friend had given him a box of laxatives as a "prank." Stan shook the thought. Every time he remembered that incident he remembered if he could survive that…he could survive anything. That was a total of five weeks of embarrassment and hiding from his friends. Still to this very day Stan carried trauma from that incident. Most anyone who heard about his mishap thought that it was a tremendously funny prank. Stan, however, did not.

Feeling his face burning up with embarrassment Stan brought himself back to the situation at hand. He knew that he would have to slowly inch down the stairwell in the dark, and that brought him great fear. He mumbled under his breath, "Don't shit yourself this time …please." He took the first step down the stairwell. Twisting his torso to the side and placing the flat of both hands on the right wall he began slowly moving down sideways. Inch, by inch. Stan noticed the smell of rotten eggs again. He felt the back of his pants quick to make sure he hadn't already failed his goal of not defecating. Stan was already terrified as he possibly could be. In his mind he kept telling himself to stay strong and that this would "Be over soon, don't be such a baby." He slowly continued forward in the dead silence of the night. Inch, by Inch, holding his breath. After what seemed like a lifetime in silence, nothing more than the sound of his soft fuzzy socks scuffing the hardwood floors as he slowly drug his feet.

Stan felt himself finally stepping off the last step onto the hardwood floor. A slight wave of relief waved through him. Now he would just have to make his way into the living room where a vast majority of everything they had was chaotically stacked. Feeling his way through the open double doorway he continued to step one foot in front of the other. Inch, by inch. Both hands were stuck directly out and in front of him now. He felt like a damn zombie from "Night of The Living Dead".

The smell of rotting eggs still permeating in his nostrils as he continued on. Inch, by inch. Waving his hands slowly back and forth, and quietly doing so he began to sense that he was about to nudge into something. "A wall perhaps? He thought to himself. Taking in a deep breath the rotting egg smell only seemed to be worse than before, he could literally taste it now. He immediately knew that he was in some sort of trouble. The feeling of death and torment grabbed his soul, paralyzing him in such a way he never felt before. He knew that it was no longer a close fear to run into something of his nightmares. It was fucking here before him, and it was real life. Stan felt his breath growing cold.

His lungs felt like they were filled with ice, and he felt

chilled to his bones. Paralyzed with his arms out like a zombie, the rooms atmosphere completely changed to that of death and despair. It was no longer a joke. Something was really going on in this place.

Stan knew this wasn't good, he was not able to make sense of any of the sensations happening to him. A virgin to an authentic paranormal experience. He began to see in the dark before him a pale white, almost holographic corpse of a nun who appeared to be floating. Her face distorted and slightly smashed in, her eyebrows dropped in anger, her flesh appeared rotted. His heart began to race at a rate he had never experienced.

He did not waste a single second trying to determine if what he was seeing was real. He absolutely knew that it was certainly there. Complete anguish and torment overrunning his mind, body and soul. Here face glowing an unnatural white tone with no eyes, just black evil, rotting holes. Stan could only think to scream to Victor, but nothing could come out. Not so much as a whisper. Stans breath completely taken away asphyxiating him. Stan could feel the absolute rage and anger from this thing across the room.

The nuns face starring him down and slowly inching towards him. Without actually using language he could tell exactly what this nun wanted…it wanted him to look her dead in her back hole eyes, it wanted his fear, it wanted to own him, it was clear the nun wanted to take his soul.

White beams suddenly blasted into the room blinding Stan. "What the fuck," Stan thought. This is it. I'm getting beamed to hell, not able to think of a single thing he had done that was so bad God would allow his soul to be exterminated from earth, also not realizing that a beam of white light usually meant heaven, not hell. The nuns face no longer creeping death towards him. She had seemingly disappeared just as fast as she came.

His body released in an instant, gasping for air Stanley

realized that a car had pulled into the driveway, the headlights blasting directly through the window into the living room in which the nun was going to eradicate his soul in. What seemed like an eternity, with time freezing still probably had happened in a matter of seconds. Stan looked through the window, he had no idea was originally there in the dark. The headlights still beaming through. The engine idling quietly. At the bottom of the windowsill on the ground Stanley could see the silhouette of the lamp he was after with the sleep sack right next to it conveniently. Immediately he bolted grabbing the lamp by its shade and the sack by its string. He flung himself towards the stairwell that he could hardly make out in the midst of the headlight beams. He dashed up the stairs faster than he had ever moved before.

About halfway up the stairs he could hear that car backing out. The sound of gravel crunching under the tires "Their turning around" he thought. "Thank god!". Stan had now made it into his bedroom where he would crawl around on all fours as fast as he could praying to find the one single outlet he could plug his nightlight into, terrified the nun might reappear to harvest his soul again. Stan managed to find his outlet in a timely manner and sooner than later he had a small dim light hardly enough to cast his shadow on the wall behind him, but at least it was something to lay next to all through the night.

Stan crawled in his sleep sack still shivering, wondering if Victor would meet the nun too. Stan did not sleep one wink. He also did not have another incident all through the night. He laid with his eyes wide open listening for anything at all. Nothing else happened.

# WAKE UP

Stan lay still in his sleep sack paralyzed with fear; he could feel the bags under his eyes drooping. By this point in the morning the sunrise had begun to pierce through the window in his bedroom, but it did not seem to help with the chill in his bones. He felt like one of them outlanders from Alaska who live with the land. This must be the how their bodies feel every night sleeping on pine needles on the tundra floor. Stan could only wonder how Vics night had gone. Stan hadn't heard so much as a flatulence echo down the hallway. Very uncommon of victor to not let everyone know he was passing ass by pushing out bombs for everyone to hear. For some reason that was still as funny to Victor as it had been when they were 5-year-old boys on the playground pointing their back ends at each other shooting methane bombs.

Stans watch beeped bringing him back to life on life's terms, just as it aways did at 6:00 a.m. every morning. He wasn't ready to move yet. He knew he would have to go wake up Victor and try to feel out the situation. But he sure as hell wasn't looking forward to having to crawl out of his safe place in his sleeping sack. Stan had not even considered that what he had experienced last night was his imagination. He knew from the very minute he walked into this house that something was 100 percent off and wrong with this place. He didn't doubt for a minute what he seen the night before was real or not. He absolutely knew this place was not normal. The ghost stories and house history from the girls at the bar only confirmed what his gut had been telling him all along.

Stan hesitantly inched his way out of the seep sack, he could see his breath even more than the day before it had to be 25 degrees. March in Michigan could be rough. Climbing to his feet he was thankful for the morning light piercing the window because the busted up used lamp had died at some point in the morning.

Shaking off his fear and fatigue Stan decided it was best to just go for it and not act like the scared little cat he was. What would Vic have to say to him if he had told him what he had experienced in the living room last night. Vic would be sure to cop it up to nothing more than the girls ghost stories getting to him.

Heart racing with fear of not knowing what was on the other side of the bedroom door waiting for him he proceeded with false confidence. Swinging the door open like a jolly ole chap he was relieved to see that there wasn't a decrepit nun waiting on the outside for him still.

Stan took in a deep breath breathing in the smell of the hardwood floors. "Much better than rotten egg smell" he thought to himself. Stan turned his head and studied the hallway towards Vics room on the left noting again that there was a large stretch of hallway with but only Vics bedroom door at the far end. Seemed like a waste of space... He noticed the door was still shut. He then looked to the right where he could partially see down the stairwell into the living room.

Not a noise or movement from that direction either. Everything appeared fine and dandy. For a split-second Stan felt a little relief. And for the first time he began to doubt himself about what he had experienced the night before. Perhaps this was just his imagination running away.

Stan slowly and quietly started down the left towards Victor's bedroom where he would then non-shalantly ask a few questions and try to determine if Victor had experienced anything completely unusual and dark himself on their first night in the hell hole. With only a few steps left Victor came out of his bedroom before Stan could reach him. "Good morning brother" said Victor as he stood face to face with Stan now.

"You look like complete shit man". "Oh jeez. Thanks man" replied Stan. "What the fuck happened to your face?" "I didn't get much sleep man; it was really cold in my room". "Yeah, we will get the heater going today, you are goanna go downstairs and get that fixed up" Stan was beginning to realize that Victor hadn't seemed to have any sort of discomfort or recognition of strangeness for the place. He was acting entirely like his usual asshole self. "I'm sure I will "replied Stan.

Both boys now walking inline to the stairwell to start the day. "We got a lot of work to get done today" said victor as if Stan wasn't already dreading being delegated to go into the basement and fix the damn furnace. Stan hadn't the slightest idea why Victor assumed he even had any sort of mechanical skills.

But victor seemed to be his usual self, so that had to be a good indicator that Stans experiences were merely figments of his wild imagination. Or are they? . Reaching the bottom of the steps Stan had noticed nothing unusual, no sort of reminders that last night was real. He had expected to see the cliché writing on the wall in blood "GET OUT" or perhaps "DIE" or even "GO NOW" just like all the horror flicks, but he seen nothing. Everything was in its cluttered mess just as the movers had left it for them.

## "BETTER THAN THE BOTTOM"

"We really should have started on this instead of going to the bar last night," said Stan. "Victor looked at him with a little grin. "But then we wouldn't have had the opportunity to meet the sexy trio. "Sexy trio?' replied Stan. "You gave them a nickname?" ha-ha both boys started laughing. Stan began to feel more like himself, and it was a bit of a relief considering the pure torment he was stuck in the past 5 hours in his sleep sack.

Vic walked right over to box that had chicken scratch writing on the side "kitchen shit". Stan had specifically remembered packing that box and it just so happened he wrapped the glass pitcher in paper for protection. "The movers had better not break our coffee pot or there is going to be hell to pay". Said Victor. Stan would not have been surprised if that coffee pot was laying in tiny pieces inside, the outside of the box was hardly shaped like a box anymore though. The corners were just about busted out on three of the four sides. Vic pulled out the big ball of newspaper. "Moment of truth". Said Vic.

Victor tore the paper off the coffee pot as if it was a Christmas present, and he was five years old again. Stan sometimes felt that Vic had stopped maturing at five years old. "BINGO!" both Stanley, and Vic had said harmoniously. "Looks like it's going to be a good day after all Stan". Victor proceeded to dig the canister of coffee out of the bottom of the blown-out box, the corners tore a little more causing the box to deflate some more. Stan was impressed the box still had some integrity left. He wasn't too worried about the loss because he had gotten the boxes for free from the back end of a run-down factory, they had lived next to while in Muskegon heights. They hated the constant noise the factory would generate 24/7 but it was mighty nice to have free access to the dumpsters out back which seemed to always have something good to take home and put to use. Both boys never felt bad about it. They didn't consider it stealing since they would utilize whatever particular item they would pull out. Afterall, they DID throw it out.

Victor had made his way into the kitchen, searching for an outlet to plug the coffee machine into. "Not a lot of outlets in this place," said Victor. Stan "You aint lyin". Stan was reaching down into the bottom of another box marked "Plates and shit" searching for two coffee mugs, any mugs at all. To Stanleys delight his search ended sooner than later where he had produced two plain black coffee mugs wrapped in newspaper. Stan could see part of the obituaries wrapping around one of the cups. "Forest Eldine 29 years of age passed over in a twinky eating contest on…."

The rest of the article was unreadable, and water stained. He thought to himself that that name had sounded oddly familiar. It must have been the guy everyone called "GUMP", or sometimes even "WOODS". "What a dork" he thought to himself completely ignoring the fact that dying at the age of 29 was still much too young.

It seemed to be a common thing in the heights... Lots of premature lives ending much too soon. Stan believed that the land had a tribal curse amongst it, going back all the way to the days the tribes ruled the land. The tribes had their land stolen by the white man. Who wouldn't want to curse them? Victor had finally found an outlet. He had used one of the boxes to prop the coffee pot on such as a corner table. Not a lot of kitchen counters existed in this old Victorian style house, mostly open cupboards and such.

As Stan sat the unwrapped cups on the home-made box counter his mind had begun slipping back to what he had seen last night. His mood immediately that of depression and fear. Every time this Nuns face came back into his mind, his whole demeanor would change again to that of anguish, and despair.

"You might want to get cracking on the damn furnace before we freeze to death in here". Said Victor. It was as if Victor knew where his mind had just wandered, and he wanted to fuel the fire. That was typical timing of Victor to further agitate a feeling and emotion that was already serious enough. "Just got to find my flashlight and toolbox "replied Stan shortly, not thrilled that he yet again been delegated to do something that he had no idea what he was doing.

Stan thought to himself for a second that he could toughen up and be a man, but he also had half the interest to call the landlord and tell him to get his deceptive ass over here and fix the utilities. Stan decided he would get it done and over with right now. He wouldn't even wait for his first cup of coffee to finish brewing, even though it had already begun. "It will be a reward" he thought to himself.

Trying to create something he could look forward to before heading into the hell. Stan walked back into the living room and began searching for the box marked "tools and shit" Victor wasn't too bright when it came to labeling boxes. He usually left it pretty vague, and he thought it was the funniest thing ever. Stan scanned the busted boxes only to find that the box he was after would be at the very top of the stack.

"Better than the bottom" he thought to himself. Stan

reached as high as he could manage without pulling a groin and grabbed the box down. He knew he was that much closer to having to embark on a mission he was terrified to do. Right inside the box plain as day was the small red toolbox his sister had bought him for his 15th birthday with a note that said "Time to be a man" he wasn't sure how to take that at the time, but he was thankful to have some basic tools. They came in handy on numerous occasions, especially when the pipe broke under the sink in their small apartment back in the heights.

Stan grabbed out his toolbox and inside of that toolbox was his 400 lumen LED flashlight he absolutely loved to use. With a deep slow breath Stan closed his eyes saying a quick prayer. "Father in heaven, please be with me and guide me into the basement of this terrifying place". It was at the exact moment both boys were startled by a loud crashing noise upstairs. "What in the fuck is that?!" yelled Victor. "This place is always making noises.

"Probably the damn kids baseball hitting the side of the house again" said Stan trying to rationalize this before his mind began slipping away again. He knew that if he were going to head down to the basement he had never been in, and work on a furnace that he had no idea how to fix, that he would have to have a rational mind before doing so. Victor slid the tiny kitchen window above the sink open, "yeah I can see them playing out there right now" Victor scowled. "Watch where you're tossing yer Fuckin balls ya brats!!". Victor slammed the window. Both boys started laughing in relief. It was almost if Victor was scared too but wasn't willing to admit it. Neither one of them could manage another episode of "Guess who's here hiding". But Victor would always play the tough guy role. After all, he was "The alpha dog" of the house.

Stan stood there in a brief spout of silence with his toolbox in his hand looking like a poignant puppy dog. "Well, you better get moving if we are goanna have any sort of heat today." Said Vic in a rushed voice. It seemed as if Vic were just as scared as Stan but wouldn't openly admit it. "On my way captain" said Stan in a fake motivated voice. Stan began walking to the far-left corner of the kitchen in silence where the basement door was located. Somehow, he had known that this was the entrance to the basement without ever being down there before. An intuitive conclusion created by his fear. He started moving his feet before his mind would try to make an excuse to get out of it. "Get moving" he non audibly told himself. Completely covered in cobwebs and was a dark brown looking color was the basement door. It looked like the color of a carpet that had dried blood on it, the kind of thing you see on them murder documentaries that tend to show the graphic crime scene photos for everyone to see.

The doorknob was covered in rust. It looked like it had the potential to give someone lock jaw if they had not been careful opening it. "I'll have a nice hot cup of joe waiting for you when you're done little buddy." Said Victor in an ass kiss kind of voice. Stan slowly turned to look at him. "Yeah, you fucking better" Stan accidently barked with a spout of anger in his voice. Typically, Vic would go off the handle if Stan had spoken to him in such a violent tone of voice. But Vic just returned a look of concern, and slightly bobbed his head back and forth.

# NO STOPPING NOW

Stan completely terrified and trying to hide his shaking hands grabbed the cold, old, rusty doorknob. This was it. He was sure he would have his soul sucked out by some demonic Prescence he believed to be in this house. "Maybe it was the guy who murdered his family" still here and full of rage. An earthbound soul, trapped for eternity. That thought was eradicated from his mind just as fast as he had imagined it. Stan turned the knob and swung the door open with a now blank mind. Immediately he was brushed by the cold drafty smell of rotting eggs and sulfur again.

Stan wasn't surprised one bit to have yet been blasted again by the smell of death. The stairwell FULL of cobwebs. He couldn't even make out where the bottom of the stairwell was actually at. Nobody had probably been down here in twenty years he thought.

 Hanging on the inside of the door was an old broom. Definitely it had been hanging here since before Stanley or Vic were even born. Probably since the sixties he assumed. Stan with his one free hand reached right through the weave of cobwebs grabbing the broom by the bottom. It took a minute to unhook from the clasp, but Stan just jiggled it up and down until the dry rotted hook actually broke right off the door. The hook made no sound as it dropped down , not the slightest clink on the floor because the cobwebs had captured it almost immediately. Again, Stan would use the length of the broom stick to spin in circles and help create a walkway just as Vic had done in the cellar entrance the night before. Circling counterclockwise he began to spin what again looked like a super massive wand of nasty ass cotton candy.

Victor still watching from across the kitchen in dead silence as Stanley hadn't even begun his first step into the stair-well began to laugh audibly. "Extracto-de-web-uz" Vic said mocking Harry Potter spells. Both boys laughed together for a few seconds as Stan wound up a tunnel. "Here I go Vic." Stan could hear the coffee pot gasping for more water, alerting him that the coffee was in fact already done by this point. "Get me that cup ready" said Stanley feeling a little more confident than before, perhaps, the laughter had balanced his brain out temporarily.

Stan began one foot in front of the other walking down the first half of the stairwell, the smell of eggs now actually created a film on his tongue. He had actually done a pretty good job weaving a tunnel, he had yet to get cobweb stuck to his hair, or body. As Stan breached the halfway point, he began spinning another cotton candy shit stick. The weight of the broom had significantly increased as it gathered cobweb material. "No stopping now" he thought to himself as he picked up some momentum in this whole process, he was all in at this point. About 33 counterclockwise spins later (he counted)

"Here we are" he mumbled under his breath he could finally see the bottom of the stairwell, a black empty room with absolutely no light. This was obviously built before basement windows and egress ports to evacuate in an emergency. He had not truly known when the last time this basement had actually seen a human being, or even a beam of light for that matter. He couldn't even make an educated guess. Stan sat his toolbox down on the very last step to dig out his 400-lumen flashlight. Stan could not see a single thing around him. A big black void, all he could feel was a vast cold draft and the musty smell of putrid basement, decomposing corpse, and rotting eggs. It was overbearing.

He had to pull his shirt over his beak with his free right hand. Stan found his flashlight at the very bottom of the box, still looking shiny and brand new just as he had hoped for. Stan took a deep breath, slowly exhaling in an attempt to try and tame his running heart rate. "You got this." "Get it done and get a cup of joe". "Today will be a good day". CLICK.

The flashlight immediately radiating light consuming the whole basement. Stan could see al the dust kicking up in the spire of light the flashlight produced. He imagined this was what it felt like on the first moonlanding. Stan squinting his eyes slowly opened them to full capacity. "This isn't that fricken scary" He mumbled under his breath. Taking a slow sweep with his head from left to right, he took an inventory of everything in the basement. Directly on the left was a bunch of old furniture he assumed, covered in dark brown stained sheets.

To the right of the furniture, was the furnace! In the exact center of the open floor plan basement. Directly to the right side of the basement was a big open space with what appeared to be a small, tiny brick room in the back, with a little wooden door, small size. It looked to be another small room. Stan was delighted that once down the stair well, the cobweb situation was different.

The majority of the cobwebs seemed to be up in the floor joists. The stairwell was much scarier than the actual basement itself. Stan now feeling a little more confident proceeded cautiously to the old gas fireplace. Covered in an inch of dust Stan began whipping the manufactures print on the side of the furnace. If this thing would give him information on how to start. He was certain that he could figure it out.

Pulling the shirt down from his nose, Stan stretched his shirt right side sleeve out over his fingertips. Wiping firmly back and forth, Stan began to uncover the manufacturing print on the side of the furnace. A sticker that was preserved in dust. "Step one- turn valve into pilot position" alongside of the first step was a visual picture showing where to turn the valve indicator. "PERFECT" thought Stan. This would be easy enough. Stan turned the indicator to "Pilot" Stan began to hear a small hiss coming from the bottom of the furnace. "Bingo" he thought. Stan wasn't the handiest man in town, but with instructions and manual print, he was just as good as the engineer who created the machine.

"Step two – with a long board match place match flame into the bottom right cylinder to ignite pilot flame. If you smell a strong odor of gas already, too much gas has been released from pilot valve. Turn valve indicator back to the off position" Stan took a deep breath. All he could smell was rotting corpse still. "I need a long match, DAMN!" Stan rifled through the small red toolbox, all he could manage to find were commonly used open end wrenches, a few different size screw drivers, both flat, and Phillips head." Stan hurriedly turned the valve indicator back to the off position. He could feel it click in; it gave him a sense of relief knowing that the gas was no longer tricking out of the ignition chamber."

"HOWS IT GOING DOWN THERE?" Victor shrieked down the stair well. It had a strange reverb in this old Michigan basement and caught Stan off guard a little.

"I NEED THEM LONG SKINNY MATCHES!" Stan said in his best version of a man's man voice. "THEN SHE'S ON" Stans voice cracked at the end making it all to knowing that he was trying to use a not natural voice and perhaps imitate a voice of a man's man he had heard in the past.

A brief moment of silence ensued. "USE YOUR DICK"

Victor yelled in a criminal voice. Stan just shook his head and tried to understand how people could produce that kind of humor day after day. He thought for a second that God had probably programmed his brain wrong upon birth. None of that sort of humor seemed to be funny to him. Why would someone insult your god given body parts? Stan had nothing intelligent to respond to that, so instead he kind of sat in silence for a brief moment. "LOOK AROUND THE BASEMENT" Victor yelled in an urgent matter. "ITS FUCKING COLD UP HERE MAN". Stan almost lost his cool for a split second barely managing to hang on to his sanity. "First you insult my penis, you force me to come down here when I know your also scared, and you treat everyone like shit" Stan mumbled this under his breath. It was moments like this that the truth of how he felt came out. Stan raised the flashlight and started scanning around the basement.

Not so much as a work bench or toolbox lay in sight. Just a bunch of covered furniture on the left side of the basement, and a small brick room roughly 12x12 on the far right, with a funny little wooden door on it. "A little hobbit door" He thought to himself. Perhaps, I should check that room Stan thought. I've yet to have anything bad happen down here yet. With a small amount of apprehension, Stan forced himself across the basement stopping three feet from the hobbit door. "I'm already here, I am man enough to complete this task. "I have to check this room." He audibly said to himself.

 Almost going into a meditative state. Stan had really pushed himself beyond his typical comfortable boundaries. I need to get this furnace fixed and prove myself to Victor once and for all. Stan reached for the small door; an even colder draft of decomposing air rushed into his nostrils. "Here            goes                    nothing"

# LEVITATION

Stan stood before the little hobbit door in compete silence, terrified of what might be on the other side. He figured if he had made it this far and hadn't been eaten alive by a demon he would be sure to be fine to enter this room and search for some long skinny matches. He took a long deep breath in and slowly exhaled. Stan turned the cold doorknob and froze, just as he had done on the basement stairs ten minutes prior.

The same exact fear of the unknown washed over his soul. Perhaps this would be the same outcome. He would open the door, knock down a few spiderwebs, find the long matches, and be on his way. Deep down he knew the chances of him actually finding the right matches for the job after this many years would probably be slim. Stan exhaled a deep breath yet again trying to slow his heart rate. He noticed his breath freezing in the air this time, he could actually hear it.

"Here goes nothing." Stan pulled the door. Nothing... Stan thought for a second. The earth seemed to stand still. Aside from the cool air that seemed to be dropping by the minute. Stan turned the knob again and pushed. The door slowly opened into the direction of the room eventually coming to a stop against the inside of the wall. "Dumbass," he mumbled under his breath." The room was completely dark, he couldn't see an inch in front of his face. He couldn't make out anything in the room, if there even was anything at all. Stan noticed the smell of carcass increase tenfold. The worst he had smelled yet. His face cringed. "Man, what in the fuck is wrong with this place." Stan raised his flashlight, his right hand slowly trembling.

Stan clicked the button not yet releasing it. One last deep breath. He hesitated to release the button. One last chance to turn around and call the landlord. After quick contemplation he knew it had to be done. If Stan backed out now it would be thrown into his face for a long time. He decided…the show must go on. As soon as he let go of that button his entire word would change unknowingly. A brief moment of complete silence and solitude. Time stood still. CLICK. The immediate second the light beamed on, all 400 lumens.

Directly in front of his face was an image he will forever remember. It was the nun. This time he could see the full figure. Standing in front of him with her head tilted up and cloak hood on. Maggots tearing away inside her mouth, the eyes completely rotted out. Black holes, full of maggots. Pale whit-ish blue deceased colored skin. The most wretched anguishing scream with the tri tone of multiple voices screeched his ears at a deafening decibel. Her mouth stretching open even more in an almost cartoon like manner.

Without having time to study her full figure he knew that she was absolutely levitating with her feet and toes pointing straight down and floating off the ground. Stans heart actually stopped. Before he could even process what he was seeing, he took off, literally jumping right out of his shoes. The flashlight hit the ground after Stan was already halfway up the stair well, never worrying once about the cobweb mess. Stanley made it up all 16 steps with big jumps. He had been an avid jogger his whole life, but never had he moved so fast. He almost flew like a bird when he later replayed the situation in his mind.

Stan slamming the door while still in a forward motion collapsed on the kitchen hardwood gasping for air. "Vic..Vic unable to catch his breath he was now in the center of the worst panic attack he had ever experienced, or ever would experience for that matter. His heart literally pounding so hard his shirt was moving 2 inches at a time. Inside the kitchen was Victor and the "sexy trio," who he hadn't heard, or notice come in at all.

They all reached down at the same time trying to comfort Stanley. "BREATHE, BREATHE, BREATHE MAN! DEEP BREATHS." "WHAT THE FUCK IS GOING ON MAN" Stan still hyperventilating had never seen Vic with such a look of concern on his face. All it did was further validate that the worst thing had truly just happened to Stan. Sarah with a calm collected look slowly reached down placing her right hand over Stans forehead speaking for the group. Stan was twitching out having a complete electrical malfunction of the brain. "Sacha Muerte, Chea, Delphiamine yatta yatta, ."

She began rambling on some sort of chant, the girls joined in the background with their eyes all closed. Vic looked absolutely terrified making direct eye contact with Stan. Stan could feel his heart rate almost slowing immediately and a wave of comfort slowly start relaxing his entire soul. "What the actual fuck is going on here" Victor yelled to Sarah.

Sarah did not acknowledge him in any way. She took her hand off of Stans head and began waiving it in front of the basement door. Some sort of witches' chant thought Stan. "This shit is actually real! He thought to himself I can't fucking believe this is real life right now." "SEAL IT AWAY, SEAL IT AWAY, SEAL IT AWAY!!" All the girls speaking in perfect harmony with absolute ferocity in their once sexy sounding voices.

The basement door began to shake ferociously back

and forth almost busting off the hinges. The most wicked tri tone screeching ricocheting amongst the walls in the stairwell. "SEAL IT AWAY, SEAL IT AWAY, SEAL IT AWAY!" All the girls speaking harmoniously. The shaking began to die down, the screeching fading away. Still Sarah held her right hand out in front of her stopping whatever the hell was trying to come through that door frame. Victor had no idea what was going on. Everything had happened too fast in the blink of an eye. Stan was paralyzed with fear/confusion.

Everything seemed to simmer to dead silence almost as fast as the chaos ensued. Stan lay on his back taking in deep breaths and exhaling slowly, he looked over at Victor who seemed to be entirely frozen and with the most terrified look stan had ever seen on his face. "Tough guys do get scared" Stan thought to himself. Sarah brought her hand down. "The seal worked". "At least for now". It will find a way out eventually. "WHAT THE FUC@#!". said Stan. The girls all looked at Stan. "You're lucky you still have your soul kid" "This house has had a demon and his mistress locked inside for the past 20 years." "The town priest sealed the demon inside the coal room downstairs twenty years ago."

"The priest wasn't strong enough to banish it back to hell". "And you my scared friend have just opened it back up." "We didn't want to tell you until today, we weren't sure how you boys were going to take it." "And what are you? The town witches?" said Vic. "Something like that replied Sarah. "We have been keeping tabs on this place for the last 10 years.

Most tenants don't even last a single night." "We thought for sure that you would leave ship after just a few hours here in the dark." "When we drove by this morning, we noticed the Toyota still parked out front." "Then we decided it was best to inform you of what has been going on in this residence before you open the coal room door." "Well, you're a little fricken late for that miss" said Victor with the most concern Stan had ever heard in his voice.

"Man, and I was dumb enough to sign a one-year lease on a property I only seen mere pictures of." Said Stanley with a tone of trouble finally getting his bearings back. "Man FUCK that lease!" Bellowed Vic. "I'm out of this place, I don't even care." "I'm over this freaky shit, you girls are probably behind all this shit anyways." "I knew that something was wrong with you girls the moment I laid eyes on ya'll." "The girls all laughed simultaneously.

"We are who saves your soul from eternal damnation and ownership to X" said Sarah. Sarah typically spoke on behalf of the whole crew; she was the Alpha of that bunch. "X? "Said Stan. "That's the demon that has been bound to this property, which is who possessed the man who killed his family." "He eventually inhabits your soul and uses your physical body to inflict death and suffering on earth." "The family who lived here before the Parkers were into dark worship." "They essentially tore a portal in the fabric of this very property where X was able to stake his claim." "He slowly tormented the family crushing their spirits and sanity. Sucking the life and light out of them." "That's how it                    all                    starts."

# COAL ROOM

"After Mr. Parker murdered his family, he took his own life." "His families souls resides in the hands of X. "He owns them all." "During the police investigation of the murder scene, they had asked the town priest to come out and bless the property due to the horrific magnitude of the murders." "Not something law enforcement usually does, but they have small town discretion." "The priest had noticed immediately that this was the work of the dark lord." "The letter X etched in blood all over the house."

"Everyone was also aware of the previous owner's affiliation with the occult." "The priest had left the premises as soon as he put the information together." "He knew the magnitude of the situation and he knew that he would have to excise the property and close the portals off." "He would later return with a Nun as his back up, a life long friend of his." "The excising almost killed the priest." "The demon was too strong, and the priest wasn't pure enough to banish him back to hell."

"The priest had a sexually deviant past." "He often caved to the desires of the flesh. X knew this, and he converted, and turned the nun on him to try and cave the desires of his flesh. The nun just wasn't strong enough to withstand X's snares. This resulted in the inability to entirely excise X back to hell. However, the priest was able to contain, and seal him into the coal room. As for the nun. She never returned home that night. Unfortunately, she became bound to the property. The nun isn't nearly as strong as X.

He uses her to roam the house and bring suffering to the temporary tenants. She turned her soul over to X. The only way to free the nun's soul, would be to banish X, and find the remains of the nun and give her a proper burial. Only then could she cross over to the light."

The room fell silent. Stan and Vic looked at each other

with complete dread in each of their eyes. "So, what do we do now", said Stan. "I would suggest you boys do not stay here anymore." "Grab your property and forfeit your lease." "If you so much as open that basement door, you will break the seal leaving X, and the nun to roam the town and take ownership of souls." "He would certainly try to create an army and wreak havoc on earth." The floor began to rumble right after Sarah spoke. The walls began shaking, the screeching, and gargling of the nun brought reality back into everyone's soul. The coffee pot fell off the makeshift table Victor had made, hot coffee splashing everywhere. "We have to get out of here before it tries to break the seal," said Sarah. If X exhumes enough energy, he could possibly over run that barrier.

The boys flew to their feet, Stans heart racing all over again. He thought to himself he would have to see a cardiologist if he made it through this. Sarah leading the crew began making their way towards the front door, everyone following closely. Victor had managed to be the last one surprisingly. Usually, he would be the type to pull people down in an emergency situation and step over their bodies. Victor hit the ground hard enough that Stan turned around. All of their stacked luggage in the living room began falling over like an avalanche, glass breaking, wood splintering. The house shook ferociously.

Stan yelled "Get up Vic we got to go!" Victor, wasting no time, rolled onto all fours grabbing at Stans hand as they both remained in motion, pulling himself up in the heat of the moment. The girls had made it out of the house and onto the deck at this point, Stan and Vic just a few seconds behind. Vic being the last one out slammed the front door with all his might.

# FOREVER CHANGED

They could hear the demonic screaming of the nun, and X inside the house. It didn't take an educated person to figure out that they were certainly trying to shake the basement door off and get out to grab revenge. The evil souls were immensely pissed, as expected of an evil entity. It didn't take an intellectual person to compute that. Stan had been surprised that the violent earthquake hadn't been enough to do just that. "We need to get a priest, right fucking now, "said Stanley . Sarah shaking her head in agreeance. "We need to go now!" "Everyone get in the car. Sarah, you tell me how to get to a priest, and I don't care who the priest is, he is going to take care of this before the town is overrun by evil.

The house was still rumbling, the screeching had slowly died down as the group left the deck and approached Vic's run-down Toyota. Everything out side of the house was completely silent and normal. Just the sound of birds chirping, morning doves to be exact. And the neighbor lady on her hand and knees in her garden with her over sized garden hat on. Victor opened the back passenger door, the girls all jumping in one after the other.

Vic closed the door and looked at Stan directly in his eyes across the car. For a split second, without any words, both boys knew that their lives would be forever changed. "Get in Stan," said Victor calmy. Both boys taking their seats and slamming the doors. Victor started the car. It seemed to start much faster than it ever had. Maybe it was his imagination.

He was just thankful that no matter how hard he beat this Toyota, it ALWAYS turned over and got him to his destination. Stan had wondered if the trip for help would even be worth it, perhaps the door would be busted off the hinges and evil left to prowl the town before they could even make it back with help. Vic slammed the car in reverse and reverse slammed out of the driveway tearing ruts in the gravel. Vic did not feel bad for the landlord. In fact, he wished he could do more to the property since the landlord had completely deceived them.

After clearing past all the behemoth pot holes on Clark street, surprised the ball joints hadn't busted, Vic spoke first. "Where is this sexually deviant priest?" "Vic", Stan said cutting him off. "Just head west on M-57 , he is right on the left of the road just passed the dollar store outside of town," replied Sarah calmly. "Did you forget I'm from the fuckin heights?" Barked Victor slowly starting to lose his cool. "Where the hell is M-57"? "C'mon Vic, you need to keep your stuff together right now, they are trying to help us help the town," said Stan urgently. "Let me drive," said Jessica, speaking for the second time only since Stan, and Vic had known her. "A girl? Driving my car,?" chuckled Vic.

"Why not," said Stan giving Victor a death glare for the first time ever. Victor could no longer see the property or the house in his mirrors anymore. He thought about it for a second. "If she crashes, it's on you Stan," said Victor under his breath giving Stan the look of certainty. Victor had thought for a second that he and Stan should just kick the girls out of the car and drive away, maybe this didn't have to be their problem. Something kept Vic from doing that and he felt influenced to go with the developing plan. Victor pulled over on the right side of the road before he put too much thought into all of this. Stan looked out his passenger window and noticed in the brick house off the road small children playing in their living room. He could see them through the big bay window. "What I would give just to be an innocent, clueless kid again" thought Stan. The reality of the situation starting to have its effect. Victor and Jessica made the switch hastily. This whole operation moving at military speed. It felt different seeing another person in the driver seat of the car that Stan and Vic went everywhere together in. Stan had never really cared to learn how to drive. He thought it was bad for the ecosystem. He was deemed a tree hugger by many people who knew his beliefs. Jessica seemed to be a good driver knowing just what to do; Stan could feel no significant differences in physics from Vic driving the car vs. Jessica. Stanley felt safe. The car fell to a silence as the motor wound up, carrying them to the town church. Quietly on the radio in the background, don't fear the reaper played softly. Stan found that a little ironic. Certainly, he feared the reaper. The reaper of souls.

" The reaper of souls taking a bologna sandwich break after a long night in the graveyard."

# HAND OF EVIL

The Toyotas engine slowly wound down as Jessica down shifted and pulled into an immensely beautiful church Stan thought. The ride ended just as fast as it started. Chesaning was an immensely small town with only one traffic light. You could run from one side to the other in just a few short minutes. Time seemed to be on their side. Now that I know evil truly exists on earth, I know that heaven exists. Being an agnostic beforehand, Stan promised himself that he would investigate the bible and what Jesus Christ has to say. He knew this would forever change his beliefs if he survived this.

He had heard it a million times. Jesus this, Jesus that. But he had always shrugged it off. It was the real deal now. His life would certainly change. Either his soul would be captured and held by the hand of evil, or the light would prevail, and he would get to better understand what the battle of good, and evil truly is. Jessica slammed the car in park just the same as Victor does, grinding and jolting noises ensued to conclude the silent two minute ride they had just engaged.

"You boys wait here," said Sarah. "It will take some convincing to get the priest back out to Clark street." "Better to let us talk with him than some out of towners." "He won't listen to you boys, he has never been the same since that night 20 years ago." Victor repossessed his driver seat in the car after all the girls had exited. Stan could tell that the girls were working up a plan to convince the priest. The priest had believed he did his job, and that god would do the rest. Deep down, he was just terrified, and didn't believe he was pure enough, or strong enough to condemn X back to hell.

Victor and Stanley sat in silence. Stanley leaned his head on the passenger window watching Victor out of the corner of his eye. Victor, with his hands slightly shaking flipped through the radio stations, never managing to decide on anything. Nothing but white noise from station to station. "This town has no good stations ma..," Before he could finish his sentence a country station came through crystal clear.

"Goanna drive mu tractor, oh yeah baby, climb up in this tractor, oh yeah, goanna chug a Busch latte, oh yeah." Stan and Vic immediately started laughing. A typical small farm town. At least it was peaceful, and quite pretty from what Stan had seen so far. Back in the heights, Stan had read an article on the town of Chesaning. Basically, the elderly of the town was waging war with the marijuana industry that had recently made way in the town, brining 2,000 plus jobs. Stan couldn't figure out why the old timers would try and reduce such a great financial, and economically beneficial opportunity like that.

Seemed to be the elders wanted to continue financially devastating the town simply because it went against their beliefs. Before the marijuana industry had arrived, the town was becoming flooded with quilt retreats and dollar stores hardly supporting the town. Either way it was a pretty town, and both Stan, and Vic had to get out of the city. The crime was rampantly increasing. Stan was tired of his car getting broke into every other night.

The police seemed to have their hands tied when it came to simple car thefts in the heights. The police force in Muskegon were all understaffed and too busy taking down the big criminals. Stan was thankful for that, but it still would leave him with a bad taste in his mouth for all the property he had lost over the years.

Victor, after fumbling through all the stations a second time, finally settled for the country station simply because it was the only station that would come in clear in this town apparently. "damnit ya'll" he said in a pretend southern accent. Both Stan and Vic laughed a little. It brought a little sense of release to laugh even the slightest bit. Probably had to do with the decrease in cortisol laughing could accomplish. "I hope that damn demon hasn't blown that door off the hinges," said Victor with a serious look in his eyes. "Have faith Vic, said Stanley. That seal should keep him in until the priest can finish him off. "Well ,well ,well, look at you...already having faith and all that." Victor shot him an uneasy look. "That's the only way to keep pressing forward is to have faith in something." "And that something,? Said Vic. "That the light will win. That the priest will send X back to hell and we can save the town of Chesaning.

"HAHAH...I just want us to get out with our asses in tact," Victor replied. "Maybe we should just put the car in drive and get the fuck out of here", said Vic again with a little urgency this time. "I don't know why this has to be our fucking problem. I don't owe this town my soul." Victors eyes bulged a little, and glassed over like a sapphire. Stan knew that look all said too well. The look of a bi polar maniac getting ready to spew. Stan had seen it a million times before and knew exactly what to expect. A complete bat shit melt down.

Victor had been forced by the Muskegon high school to under go a few psychiatric evaluations in order to determine if he was sane enough to attend school. Vic had decided in a fit of rage one day to rip Mr. Harrigers television of the wall mount and throw it out of the window into the court yard. IT absolutely terrified the class, and Victor went down as a hulk legend. Nobody messed with him after that. When the superintendent asked him why he did it, he admitted to them that he couldn't control it , and that he was upset it was sloppy joe day for lunch when he had initially thought it was taco Tuesday.

The school system by protocol had him evaluated by the professionals. Instead of getting expelled, it was ordered that he take a medication daily that would help balance him out. I don't think it works to well, especially since he doesn't seem to actually take it. Stan had seen Vic pretend to swallow the medication, and then throw it in the trash can in 1st hour. Sometimes Vic would sell it for a few extra bucks. He would crush it up and sell it as cocaine. It was usually the frat boys who were stupid enough to buy it for a ridiculous price at that. Stan decided to try another tactic to try and hastefully redirect Vic..

Maybe he could tell a joke and get Vics mind away from the situation at hand. "Want to hear a good joke, man?" Stan said with a grin. Victor looked at him making no expression at all, just glaring directly into Stans eyes with a look that insinuated he didn't care about anything at all. That look scared Stan sometimes, he was sure that Vic had to potential to go completely postal some day. Victor had even mentioned a hit list a few times under his breath during a fit of rage, Stan just hoped that he wasn't on the list when that time came.

"How do you know a college boy has been in your yard?". Vic continued his death glare. "The trash is empty, and your dog is pregnant." Victor shook his head side to side and slightly sighed. " How does it feel knowing you just insulted yourself? Stan humbly laughed. " Of course you would say that." Vic fist bumped Stan on his right shoulder and forced a smile. "Thanks for trying bud." Stan nodded his head shooting Vic a serious look of concern. Stan could tell it took everything in Vic to muster them words. Stan knew that Victor appreciated his companionship deep down. After all.

Stan was the only person on planet earth who stuck by Victor and could tolerate him. For that, Vic was grateful, but he wasn't always good, or genuine about showing appreciation. Stan looked in the rearview mirror, he could see the main entrance to the church still. "A peaceful little gateway into eternal pe..." The double stained glass doors blasted open. Jessica came out first holding the doors open. Sarah and Maggie had the priest hog tied, and gagged. He was a lot smaller than Stan had thought. Just a wee little priest. Sarah had him by the legs, yellow extension chord wrapping him up like the throat of a noose. Maggie had the upper torso. Maggie was a bit more athletic than the rest of the girls, it made sense she would have the bulk of the load. The priest was squirming back and forth, his face was flushed red. The kind of red that concerns a doctor who in turn gives a person twelve different blood pressure medications and a pacemaker when maybe they just need a little exercise and to stop eating cheeseburgers everyday. The girls barely managing to keep him still, continued to lug him in the direction of the car, only a mere 2 feet off the ground, they barely had him. But, they did have him.

"Ahh fuck!" said Victor now realizing in the driver side mirror what was coming towards them. "Pop the trunk!" said Stanley not even realizing what he was saying. An accomplice to a kidnapping . Not the kind of thing you would expect from someone who was on the brink of accepting Christ.

"What do you mean pop the t…." "POP THE DAMN TRUNK VICTOR!" Victor reached down on the left side of the floorboard and pulled the trunk tab, he had accidently pulled the gas cap tab as Stan noticed that opening as well. THUMP . The priest was now in the trunk of the Toyota. The girls where manic and yelling at each other. "Take his gag out Mag!" Maggie reached down and slammed the trunk , the priests head was up during their brief discussion , he had been also trying to negotiate taking his gag out, but nobody could hear anything. The trunk had come down on his melon knocking him out cold.

Everyone sat in silence for a second. The priest made no thudding, or screams. Stan could only hope the poor guy was still breathing. "Get the fuck in girls!" said Victor. The girls piled in the back seat all panting and out of breath. "Get back to the house!." "Go, go, GO!" The tires of the Toyota chirped like a bird that got its goodies stuck on the corner of the perch bar. Victor didn't waste anytime backing up, he drove straight forward off the parking lot and into M-57 . Right through the grass. Stan was surprised the front wheels carried them through that, especially with the ground being frozen from the winter still covered in frost.

Nobody said a word, the roaring of the engine speaking for everyone. Stan took a quick look around to see if anyone had witnessed the kidnapping he had no idea would happen. Next to the church was a dollar store. Their were a few old people getting out of their cars and into their walker. They appeared to have not seen, and definitely did not hear the kidnapping. Stan let out a deep breath. "What just happened!" "We had to take him by force. As soon as we walked in he hit the floor, and was crawling under the pews," said Sarah. "So we bagged the son of a bitch." "He ain't letting the town down on my watch." Sarah and the girls had a mischievous look in their eyes with a slight undertone of satisfaction.

"But why would he start crawling under the pews right away." Said Victor curiously. "Not every day a pair of witches come into the town church," replied Sarah very matter of factly. "SO YOU ARE A FUCKING WITCH!" "I TOLD YOU STA.." " WE ARE WHITE WITCHES!" Sarah overtook Vics excitement, before he took it too far. "We only do good things for people, and we believe we can make great change in the community for the better." Sarah looked at the other girls who nodded in agreeance.

"The priest doesn't like ANY witches, he thinks we are all just evil." He never lets us in on Sundays and Wednesday church sessions to mingle amongst the town. He always closes the door in our face, and we eventually stopped going.

# A WITCH IS A WITCH

"A witch, is a witch" said Victor. "You can't blame the guy too much, I have never heard of good witches." The car rolled to the first and only red stop light in the town of Chesaning. Vic was usually good at remembering directions and Stan trusted fully he would reverse the way they had got there. Stan had thought if Stan had more patience, he could've surely took directions from Sarah on how to get to the church in the first place. Stan looked out the window and the car sat silent for a moment besides the graceful tapping of the cars blinker. Nobody spoke. To the left was a brick building with an ATM outside, he was sure that it was a bank. To the right of the light was a little jewelry store. Stan could see two great beautiful diamond lined clocks gleaming in the sill.

THUMP, THUMP, THUMP!    The priest began banging on the inside of the trunk, screaming a muffled pathetic scream. The priest must have spat the gag out of his mouth. Vic spun the tires, taking a hot turn to the right before the light was green thinking how he could have went right on red a long time ago. The thudding silenced again by a much larger bang, no more screams. The priest surely hit his melon yet again when Victor brake checked him.. "Don't you kill that man!" said Stan urgently. " The last thing we want is a dead priest in our trunk, and a demon waiting to feed on the souls of the town." "The priest is our only hope." "I fuckin know that Stan!" "It fucking scared me…okay" Victor almost never would admit when he was scared. That was a new one for Stan.

We need to speed this thing up and get back to the house on Clark street right now." Chimed Sarah. "No shit sherlock" said Vic . " And just what are we goanna fucking do with the priest when we get there?!" Sarah hesitated for a second.."well …we are gunna" "We are goanna send him in the house." " He won't have a choice." "And just what the fuck are we supposed to do ? sit outside and pray?" Victor was definitely about to go into rage mode. Stressful situations eventually pushed him to the limit, and it was sure he would have a bi- polar meltdown during this exorcism. "Everything is going to be just fine, we will wait outside ." "I have faith the priest will take care of X once and for all." Stan spoke in a calm tone.

Stan was definitely scared, but didn't see much of a point in getting paranoid and angry. This situation was already bad enough. They were in the fight whether they wanted to be, or not. "You and that faith shit Stan." Victor had a disgusted look on his face. The trunk began thumping again, and little screams seaped through the back seats. " I don't see how this is going to work".. Victor said in a pessimistic tone. "Two more blocks to go Victor , step on it!" Sarah said. The little Toyota huffing and puffing as Vic shifted gears. 50 in a 25 was definitely enough to make them all look suspicious, but it was not that un common in Chesaning to see a car full of youngsters flying down the side streets.

Vic squealed into the driveway sideways throwing gravel into the neighbor's semi connected driveway. Stan seen the old woman's head pop up from across the yard. She had a sun hat on and was weeding a beautiful flower bed. Stan thought it looked marvelous, and it brought some faith to the situation. How could something so beautiful exist alongside of something so heinous and dark. Stan had already promised himself that when they came out of this, he would be a man of God, and take joy in the fruitful things of life. No more material fascinations.

The car skidded to a forceful halt; gravel pinged on the under garments of the Toyota. "Now what! Said Victor urgently as he slammed the shifter into park." " I don't want that old lady across the yard to call the police on us." The trunk was still thudding. "HELP, HELP, I'LL GIVE

YOU WHATEVER YOU WANT." They could hear the priest trying to bargain. The old lady looked back down gracefully and continued to weed the flower bed, it was then they noticed the headphones on her head. She was probably listening to church hymns Stan thought. "Don't worry about her ,she probably can't even see this far and she definitely can't hear us" Sarah.

Victor reached down and popped the trunk remembering he had already popped the gas cap open earlier. Everyone got out of the car and hastily went to see the damage Vics driving had done to the cargo.

The priest still tied up squinting his eyes, and blood trickling down from his left eyebrow. "PLEASE, PLEASE!" he pleaded. "I'll do anything.." Sarah grabbed him by the collar. "Your goanna go kick that demon in his ass, and send him back to hell." She gave him a piercing look showing him that he definitely had no say in this. "But I am not stro.." "YES ,YOU ARE!" Sarah screamed in his face. Stan had was beginning to feel sorry for the priest. A man of God tied up in the back of a car being forced to go battle an evil force that had already gave him a fight 20 years ago.

Sarah not so discretely pulled out a switch blade knife holding it at her side for the priest to see but low enough the neighbor might not notice. "Okay...okay" he said. He began to pray under his breath. "NOW!" said Sarah yanking him up and out of the trunk to his feet. "OKAY OKAY!" good lord.

The priest took a deep breath and brushed the dust off his britches. Maggie handed him her new hanky out of her back pocket. The priest wiped the bood off of his brow. Beads of sweat now began to roll down his brow and mix with the blood making a light pink colored liquid. Stan thought it almost looked like cheap fake blood/

"The town is depending on you." "You have to do this for everyone innocent that is unknowing in this town priest." Said Sarah. The priest nodded his head with his eyes shut and eyebrows squinting exhaling slowly. "I will need back up he said." Sarah shook her head and smiled big. "That's all me." She pulled out a rosary from her pocket. She held it up and it shimmered in the sunlight. "You just tell me what to do, and I will do it." Stan looked up at the house. Not a single vibration or noise came off the property. He thought that maybe X and the nun had already escaped wreaking havoc on the small town of Chesaning. The thought gave him chills.

He thought about having to get in the Toyota and drive as far away and as fast as possible, but even Stan knew you couldn't out run evil. You had to eradicate it entirely. The clouds began to cover the direct sunlight, casting darkness amongst the town of Chesaning. The white birch tree in front of the house began to creak and sway back and forth. Just like out of a horror movie Stan thought. How cliché. Sarah standing right in front of the priest put her hands on each of his shoulders as they locked eye contact. "You got this." She said in a soft motherly voice. "Lets go."

He started walking, signing the cross on his chest before exhaling another long deep breath. Stan noticed bruising starting to show on his forehead. Stan was worried he might not be in his best strengths to fight a powerful demon. Sarah and the priest walked slowly in sync up the deck stairs. A black hawk swooping over the roof of the house cawing in a echoing voice. Stan looked over to the neighbors yard. The neighbor was still weeding and she looked up again, this time she smiled big and waived. At least Stan knew that the neighbors were decent people.

# FORCED AT THE BLADE

The priest reached the final step on the deck. He slowly turned and looked at Sarah. " Are you sure?" he said softly. " You can do this, you are stronger than you know" "The town needs you" The priest looked at the house and took one final deep breath. "okay.." Sarah placed her hand on the door knob. The rusty old doorknob that was incredibly cool to the touch. All the blinds were shut, they had no idea what they could be walking into. It was dead silent. "Here we go" she said surely. Stan watched with the rest of the crew as Sarah opened the door slowly.

The priest looked petrified. Stan couldn't help but feel sorry for the guy, he had just been kidnapped, knocked out twice in the trunk, and now he was being forced at the blade to fight a demon that almost took his soul 20 years prior. Thunder echoed softly in the distance, reminding Stan just how small he was on this planet. Sarah stepped inside. The priest followed. Then the door shut softy behind them. Stan thought for sure the demon would come tearing out of the door as soon as they opened it ,screaming it's wretched tri tone scream of agony and anger. But it was just as if two completely normal people had just walked through a door to normalcy.

"He's fuckin toast man.." Victor said in a hoarse voice. "Something feels wrong."

The priest opened his eyes. He took in the smell of sulfur mixed with hardwood floor. He slowly looked from left to right. The living room was in shambles. A smashed Television, a picture of Victor with his eyes burned out lying on the floor. Splinters of wood lie everywhere; the furniture had been annihilated. The priest began to feel the air thicken. His heart rate flaring up, his face becoming flushed. He slowly raised his chin looking up from the ground in disbelief that he was actually back again twenty some years later. All the nightmares were true, he was back again. The priest began trembling as he faced forward looking into the kitchen with terrified eyes. The nun slowly came around the corner grinning. She looked just like she did 20 years prior when he came into battle with her. She appeared entirely human, but the priest knew that was a trick. She smiled at him a friendly smile as she slowly came around the corner of the basement door in full view. The priest noticing her breasts hanging out of her unbuttoned shirt. Old feelings came rushing back in like he had been injected with adrenaline.

He forced himself to look to her forehead instead of her breasts. He knew not to look at her breasts, or her eyes directly for that matter. "Where is x?" said Sarah calmly. The priest began to feel weak in the knees, sweat and blood dripping from his forehead. He is coming don't worry. She said seductively unbuttoning the rest of her gown dropping it to the floor with a mischievous smile. Thunder began to rumble outside, the priests heart rate fluttering just as fast as it did the last time he was here. Old trauma ran in like an injection from the doctor. He could feel the evil pumping through his veins.

The ambient light from outside immediately darkening an already dark room. The thunder was moving in. "Hi priest" said the nun with a little giggle. "It's been a while." The priests' eyes dropped to her nude body as she gently grabbed her breasts squeezing them together for him to admire. The priest shot his eyes back above her , he was beginning to breath heavy. Rain started pouring down echoing on the tin roof. It sounded like hail. The nun began slowy, and seductively walking towards the priest.

Sarah began giggling in sync with the nun. "I told you I would get him here, she said." " I knew you couldn't resist me" said the nun. "You've always had eyes for my body." "SINNER! " she said cackling. The priest began shaking tremendously barely able to stand. His knees began to buckle, he hardly managed to stand. The nun stopped in front of him. He looked directly in her eyes. They looked just as beautiful as they always had to him. For a minute he felt the sorrow of losing her, and knowing what he seen now was just a trick. She grabbed him in by the crotch. "You've always wanted me" she whispered in his ear. "Why don't you take me." The priest jumping back screaming "Let the blood of Christ cover you! Let the!.. Sarah knocked him on the head with a splintered board from the broken dresser. The priest dropped to the ground immediately thumping the corner of his head on the hardwood. His brow was now split another 3 inches, blood began running all down his face. He gurgled and gasped for air.

# GET IN THE CAR

"Get in the car! Said Victor. "It's fuckin storming away on us and we are all just sitting around like some sort of slug on a log waiting for something to happen" Victor pulled the driver side door open and hopped into the driver seat. Stan "C'mon ladies, it will be okay." "We will just wait for this all to be over I guess" The girls piled into the back of the car, and Stan grabbed the passenger seat feeling a little sense of relief to be out of the rain. Ten minutes had passed since their arrival with everyone just waiting outside in awkward silence . The sky darkened drowning out all the sunlight. Thunder ricocheted through the town, and the ground rumbled. "Look at them fucking clouds man!" "That CANNOT be good!" Victor pointed out of the windshield towards the house. Black swirling clouds began to spiral clockwise with twists of gray. It was as if the storm had singled out the house on Clark St. and it was raining just on the property. The rest of the sky around it was pale grey drowning out the sun. Stan looked over to the neighbor's yard. She was still sitting in her flower bed weeding. She made eye contact with Stan again and waved with a big smile on her face. Stan waived back pretending everything was normal. How could this lady be so peaceful and unconcerned he wondered?

"I wonder how it's going in there," said Stan cautiously not sure if he really wanted to know the answer. Maggie, and Jessica didn't make a peep. They sat still watching the storm above the house in amazement. Victor flipped the radio back on. The radio screen read "Cellphone Tumor" by Demonfband . Stan flipped the radio back off. "Are you serious man?!" "This isn't the time to be listening to music and pretending nothing is happening. We need to pay attention to every little detail right now, we need to be able to get in there and help out if things go wrong... "Oh fuck you Stanley you're just a ..." Stanley completely lost it as he swung his door open. "Fuck you man! I am tired of.."

BOOM! The front door flew open on the house. Everyone dropped dead silent. Everyone's eyes piercing the doorway . jaws dropped. Dead silent. The storm had started swirling the opposite way as if it was reversing, being pulled back into the high atmosphere, almost vanishing as fast as it had appeared. Stan began shaking uncontrollably with apprehension. "Damn that was fast", said Victor excitedly. Nobody else said a word. Sarah came through the door first, she had her left arm around the priest who was stumbling and covered in blood head to toe. He clung to her side for support. He barely had his eyes open, they appeared to be almost swollen shut. They stopped at the top of the deck.... Dead silence. The priests head bobbed and weaved back and forth as he tried to hold it up. Slowly he began to raise his right hand and barely managed to give a thumbs up.

Stan fell to his knees, and everyone began cheering! "You fucking did it!!! Said Victor beeping his horn. Maggie and Jessica began to cry. "The town will be complete again!" said Jessica in a choked voice. Sarah smiled big with a look of victory. The neighbor still sitting in her flower garden weeding gave another big wave, with a big smile on her face. She knew the priest very well and was an avid member of his church. But nobody else knew that. She couldn't possibly even recognize anyone from that far away anyways thought Stan.

"What now?" said Vic. "Grab a side and help get him down the steps,", said Sarah. "We will get him back to the church and I will heal him up." "Then you boys will be free to get back to a normal life." "HAHA! Like that'll fucking happen", said Vic. "How you plan on healing him up anyways? With your fancy white witch shit?" Victor got out of the Toyota and slammed the door behind him. "This whole situation feels fucked up". "Victor grabbed the priest by his left side, together with Sarah they managed to hobble the priest down the stairs, and load the priest into the back seat. Victor had half the motivation to stuff him back in the trunk due to the amount of blood that saturated his shirt and spiled down his face.

The priest didn't make a peep as they loaded him into the back of the Toyota. Stan was worried he had some significant head trauma since he didn't really seem coherent, and his eyes were an odd shade of orange instead of the usual white cornea. Victor and Stanley had no idea that they just got fooled into kidnapping the priest so X could finish him off . X would certainly use his power through the priest to expand his course of evil, the followers of the church would do anything he asked of them…and X knew that.

It was the perfect plan twenty years in the making. "Do you think we should take him to the emergency room," said Stanley in a concerned voice. Victor shut the door closing the priest in the car and out of the conversation. "And tell them what Stan? That we fucking kidnapped him, knocked him out multiple times. "Oh and don't forget he got his ass whipped by a demon who was trying to over run the town?" "What happened in there anyways Sarah," said Stan, the curiosity now getting the better of his thoughts.

"The priest did his job, and that's all that matters." "Lets get him to the church." "Jessica and Maggie why don't you guys help Stan get this place cleaned up some." "If you would, Victor could you please get the priest and I back to the church so I can fix him up, tomorrow is his weekly sermon and it will be a great opportunity for him speak his word to the entire town"?

"Guess I don't mind if it gets me away from cleaning this hell hole house." "Hop in and lets go, this guy is bleeding like a stuck pig all over my car." Victor looked back at the priest who gave him a smile. " I like you" the priest said in a gargled hoarse voice. "That makes one of you", victor chuckled. Sarah got in the passenger seat. For a second victor was aroused to have a woman in his front seat for once. Victor seemed to be returning to his asshole self now knowing that the situation had played out well.(or so he thought) Victor probably would be no more humble after this experience, it surely would take much more to open his eyes. Some people were like that unfortunately. It would probably take death for Victor to have an awakening, and even then, that might not be enough to change him. Victor put the car in reverse and backed down the rut he had created when they fled the house earlier, and in a few brief seconds the car sped off the sound of the engine growing distant as the rest of the crew stood in silence.

# SUNDAY SERMON

The priest stood before his flock of sheep with an amber tint to his bloodshot eyes both arms raised to their max. The sun disappeared behind the clouds leaving a grey tint behind all the stained-glass windows behind him. The pale grey of the sky shadowed the entire town of Chesaning. This was the first time the sun wasn't charging down through the windows casting spires of light onto the priest. On the large scale crucifix pinned to the wall directly behind the priests podium, Jesus was missing. The town probably believed it was under renovation. Before him in the front pews sat Sarah, Jessica, and Maggie for the first time ever. Almost the entire town was kneeled before the priest. They all sat eager to hear his words today, for they fully trusted him and would abide by all the laws he would lay down in the name of the "lord"

The priest spoke, his voice a completely different tone than ever before, a evil smile in his eyes. "Today is the turning point in all you've come to know." The crowd sat in complete silence, a pause between his sentences. "Today I will change your hearts." "Today the old you, will perish for eternity."

Victor and Stan sat in the back. They both slowly turning their heads towards one another, eyes wide, jaws dropped….it all started to come together for them. "Today," said the priest. "You will ALL turn over your souls in the name of the LORD."

*If you have read this far you have made it through the first episode of Far Beyond Fear, a comedy/ horror short story series with a non fiction message to decipher. Or you have simply flipped to the end of the book and decided to read this page first you silly willie. I hope you have had a good laugh, or perhaps this was even spooky for you to some degree? I hope so....This is just the start of a long series full of darkness that is reprieved with light. There is a story to be told of truth even in the midst of a fictional story. A truth of good and evil. They both exist. Everyday, all day. How do you choose to approach life? Do you believe we are just a scientific miracle who just so happens to have spiritual curiosity? Or do you believe we are created in the image of a high power? I personally choose to believe in Jesus Christ as the savior to humanity. I don't wish to be confused with organized religious cults. It is my opinion that often times a person is steered away from the church due to "not being accepted", " you drink and smoke you're going to hell" etc...I feel that many churches have become self-righteous and can sometimes do more harm than good. The Jesus I know is loving and forgiving and he wants EVERYONE no matter who you are or what you do, to talk to him. Never let anyone on earth tell you that you are going to hell...it is NOT their place or decision, and if they are the type of person to preach that to you than they aren't a true representation of the loving forgiving Christ I know. If anyone in the church thinks they are better than any other sinner, they are in the wrong mindset. He is not going to condemn me to hell for drinking coffee and reading comic books. I know many people who have had one bad experience with the church and immediately develop hatred towards them all which ruins their ability to connect completely. Them self-righteous people are not the image or reflection of a person who is a believer in Christ. They completely paint the wrong image. WOLVES IN SHEEP CLOTHING. A good brother and sister will show you that the lord wants you to talk to him and that he loves you, despite what you have done in life, or who you are. A good brother or sister will welcome you with loving open arms. A safe place when the darkness tries to drown out your light in life. Some people when they become self-righteous completely miss the loving connection to their higher power. I've sat with people who have not missed a single day of church in 25 years but then turn around and tell me that they don't pray much throughout the day… and that God only saves those who do good and never miss church. It is the people like that who unfortunately miss the big picture completely and push away their brother and sister. My hope is that you can take the good away from my series and have a good laugh. Consider when reading these stories that they aren't entirely fictional. Get deep into the story and picture it as reality. Witness the battle of good and evil. Because at the end of the day, it is NOT fiction. It happens right before our eyes every single day.*

Made in the USA
Columbia, SC
05 August 2023

21256185R00052